The Princess Who Wouldn't Come Home

The Princess

Who Wouldn't Come Home

written by

Irving Finkel

and

illustrated by

Jenny Kallin

*To Ruby!
The great artist!
With best wishes
from
Irving.
April 20th
2011.*

K&B

Kennedy & Boyd
an imprint of
Zeticula
57 St Vincent Crescent
Glasgow
G3 8NQ
Scotland

http://www.kennedyandboyd.co.uk
admin@kennedyandboyd.co.uk

Text Copyright © Irving Finkel 2008
Illustrations © Jenny Kallin 2008

ISBN-13 978 1 904999 80 5
ISBN-10   1 904999 80 8

All rights reserved. No part of this publication may be reproduced, stored in a retrieval system, or transmitted in any form or by any means, electronic, mechanical, photocopying, recording or otherwise, without the prior permission of the publishers.

This book is dedicated
to the memory
of Angela Jill Brice

(July 20th 1954-August 24th 2007)

Huge reader
great healer
and
our
beloved
wee
sister

❧ 1 ❧

Doors had actually slammed in the Palace on the afternoon that the Princess finally departed. The Queen, predictably, refused to come down and say goodbye at all, and the others had been instructed to stay in their rooms. Her Father alone had seen her safely into the coach, murmuring to the horses and patting her own cheek too through the lowered window. At the last minute he had discreetly passed her a heavy old purse of velvet. King Darius raised a hand in farewell, made a thumbs-up sign and added a wink of encouragement. And then... she was gone...

To those who know about such things it was perfectly obvious at once that she was a Princess, although hardly anybody in England ever told themselves she *must* be, or discovered exactly which country she came from, or which particular King was her Father.

As this account begins the Princess in question had just moved into a ground floor flat somewhere in London. When she saw it for the first time there wasn't much furniture and it was hard to tell what colour the paint was supposed to be. Despite these disadvantages she knew at once that it would suit her perfectly. The next morning at ten o'clock prompt the perspiring estate-agent padded up to the front door and handed her the keys. *Her own keys*! The Princess dumped her bags and boxes in the hall, opened all the windows, and walked up and down plotting and planning. More than a little white paint was called for, she thought. She considered her finances, locked everything up again, and went off to the builders' suppliers in the high street.

Anyone looking through one of the freshly-washed windows that afternoon might have seen the Princess in a red head-scarf pirouetting round the room to her portable radio, waving a roller. The rooms were transformed. Hours later, hardly recognising her own grimy hands, she dined off a mug of instant soup, two apples and a small bar of chocolate. With the windows closed against insects the paint smell was overpowering, so she decided to sleep on the old leather sofa that someone had kindly deposited in the hall outside. Although princesses tend to be racked by insomnia when there is so much as a pea under the mattress she was not that type, and she fell asleep instantaneously, holding her new door key.

In the morning she moved all her possessions in from the hall and spread them about where they looked most comfortable. It felt a bit sparse, she thought. She would need a rug or a bit of carpet. A little more furniture, and certainly some pictures for the walls.

Later that first afternoon the Princess passed an Oxfam shop with lots of useful-looking things in the window. She went in. There was an interesting picture that was not too expensive. Getting it home with her other purchases, however, was a struggle. The back of the old frame was covered with torn brown paper, and, as she was crossing the road, the wind suddenly whipped up and ripped it right off. The picture inside billowed out and soared up into the sky, vanishing in a moment over the roofs. Before she knew what had happened, all she had left was one empty picture frame. *Bother*!

The Princess was cross with herself, and stomped up the path with an unmistakable frown. She put down her shopping in the kitchen and looked around for somewhere to put the annoying frame. The rubbish bin was too narrow, and there was nowhere else. There was, however, a convenient nail in the wall left by a previous tenant, so she looped the wire over it and straightened the frame roughly against the plaster.

Then the door bell rang.

'Bother,' thought the Princess again.

The person at the door looked confused. He was shabbily dressed and generally untidy, with papers stuffed in his pockets.

'I see you have moved in. *Good*. Hello. Look, do you by any chance have a pencil sharpener?' he enquired. 'I'm composing and my last pencil keeps breaking. It's infuriating.'

The Princess thought about the contents of her boxes. She didn't have a pencil sharpener. There was the kitchen penknife, of course. The composer took it gratefully.

'Nice picture,' he commented, pointing with a languid finger.

He left. The Princess inspected her picture frame. It did look interesting against the white grainy surface. It was now a picture of a wall, she thought.

'Nice picture,' he commented

There was lightness and sunshine in the flat, and the Princess was happy in her white rooms. For many days she spoke to nobody, but lay on the floor reading poems or the advertisements in the local paper, writing in her diary, or inventing new kinds of sandwiches, such as sardines with cherries. (There was no one to be critical or rude, even if the strange combinations were disastrous.) She bought a rickety chair, a pretty lamp that didn't work very reliably, and an old green-painted ironing board. Gradually the space around her became closer, and her own.

Remembering her penknife she tripped up the worn stairs clutching a small package, to visit her neighbour. There was no response to her knocks, but she knew from bumps on her ceiling that the composer must be home. Undaunted, the Princess turned the handle and peeped around the edge of the door. The room was the complete opposite of her own, awash in paper, music, recordings and unidentifiable musical instruments. Her intriguing neighbour was seated with his back to the door, bent over a worn-looking piano keyboard placed on the table. There was no sound at all. He was playing steadily through a piece of music, stopping once or twice to replay certain notes more emphatically, or scribble on his sheet. When he had finished his visitor coughed quietly. He turned around and looked at her without surprise or recognition. The Princess acknowledged his performance by clapping her hands so softly that she made no sound herself. The composer bowed as best he could while remaining seated.

'A-ha!' he cried. '*You*! Your penknife! Now, *where* did I put it…?'

'I've brought you a new pencil-sharpener in exchange,' said the Princess.

The composer emerged from under a pile of papers brandishing the knife dangerously. The Princess stepped back.

'I always know where everything is in this room,' he said, contradicting himself. 'People come in here and express incredulity, but they don't intimidate me.'

'People truly come in here?' said the Princess. 'You surprise me.'

He offered the open knife to her, but handle first, like a gentleman. The Princess inspected it critically.

'You've got wood and lead smears all over it,' she said. 'Everything will taste of pencils.'

'It's good quality graphite,' said the composer defensively. 'I can never write a note with a biro or one of those felt-tip things. First-rate pencils only. I should imagine they're rather nourishing.'

'I was brought up never to chew writing implements of any kind,' remarked the Princess.

'Would you like me to play you something else?'

'I should be delighted. Something more austere.'

The composer bent once more over his skeleton keyboard. It was relaxing being treated to inaudible music. The keys themselves made a faint and hypnotic flicking, like a distant typewriter. The Princess watched his long white fingers at work and she fell into a daydream, sitting in the pale sunshine streaming through the window. It became clear after a while that the composer had forgotten his guest entirely. She stood up very quietly and slipped out of the room, holding her penknife.

A day or two later her upstairs neighbour was just leaving the house as the Princess opened the front door.

'What is your *name*, incidentally?' he asked her. He was wearing a long scarf and an ill-judged hat. He probably thought it made him look like a composer, she said to herself.

'You've never told me yours.'

'Don't be infantile.'

'My name is Irena Natasha. I am incapable of being infantile. I am a Princess in hiding. Plain clothes.'

'Oh, I see… Well, I'm the *Mar*-quis of *Queens*-bury. Otherwise known as Belshazzar. Writer of great but unrecognised music.'

'Your lack of perception as to my ancestry does not astonish me. How could an *apprentice* musician be expected to be in tune with such things?'

'True. I apologise, your royal highness.'

'Do get up please. The phrase "Your Royal Highness" takes capital letters, and that should be reflected in your pronunciation, but I'll forgive you.'

She shut her own door gently but firmly. The composer proceeded meditatively down the front steps. He had, of course, never met a Princess personally before, and wasn't quite convinced that he had done so now, but the idea of living in the same house as even a possible princess was quite inspiring. And there *was* something about her…

'I'll write her a special piece of music,' he thought, 'something wonderful, regal, beautiful…'

He hummed reflectively.

∽ 2 ∽

Princess Irena was out on one of her walks. She moved swiftly and determinedly, and anyone watching her would have assumed she was hurrying to an appointment, but in reality she was just wandering. Going off on her own somewhere to see what might happen was something that she could never get away with in her old life. Or going out in the rain, in particular: the Palace staff would have run scolding after her with giant umbrellas, or a sedan chair. It was raining beautifully now. She didn't have an umbrella, but preferred a floppy hat like an upside-down goldfish bowl, which kept her hair dry although it didn't do much for the rest of her. She was wearing her poncho, a sort of smock with a pouch in the front, over a long skirt. The poncho was dark blue and now even darker, as it was drenched. Her stride slowed into a damp, hesitant plod, and she turned for home, thinking of hot chocolate.

She was wearing her poncho ...

The Princess liked artists, and secretly hoped that, wearing her poncho, she looked like one. She was (not to reveal any secrets) rather a good painter herself, but extremely reticent about it. Painting happened to be the only thing about which she was truly shy. She was even a bit shy about her drawings, although she sometimes used to let her brothers and sisters see them if they wanted. In the flat she had a dark-blue beret which she thought made her look even more like an artist than the poncho, but she wouldn't wear it in the street in case a passing Frenchman asked her the way. (Not that her spoken French wasn't impeccable, of course. There had been ample governesses.) The Princess liked going to art galleries to look at the pictures, and she also liked reading about artists. Photographs sometimes showed them working in a smock like her poncho, usually smeared with paint and turpentine, with brushes and tubes stuffed into the front pocket. She always kept a pad of white paper and several pencils in the pouch, so that she could do some drawing when she felt like it. The pad had all gone soggy.

Later that afternoon there was a formal-sounding rap at the door. The Princess was preoccupied scribbling in her diary, and felt reluctant to get out of the deep and sagging armchair in which she was curled up. The second knock prompted her to make the effort. She peeped through the window, and saw a burly shiny motorbike tied up at her gate.

'Perhaps it's a parcel,' she thought.

It wasn't, however. A willowy young man in immaculate livery with frilly cuffs stood at the threshold, holding a bunch of flowers and a crash helmet, although without his customary rapier.

'Your Royal Highness…,' he said tentatively, 'your Father… wants you to come home.'

'Nothing doing,' said the Princess promptly.

'But, your Royal Highness…'

'*But nothing*. I am tired of snow and I don't like the conversations. I want sunlight and solitude.'

'But… what shall I tell His Majesty?' The equerry turned his head slightly, poignantly. 'I've come all this way… brought your travelling cloak and everything…'

'Kindly inform him that I have become a recluse and that shortly I am going to become an artist. State also that from now on I will countenance neither emissaries nor flowers. I admit I sent him one message. I saw a sentimental poster in the Post Office saying "They'd love to hear from you," and in an undisciplined moment I weakened. This does not imply an intention to return. There are other Princesses to hand. I've got two perfectly marketable sisters, remind him.'

'Well, this is a fine thing. I'll lose my bet with... I mean, you are *needed* at home on all sides... The royal hounds, let me tell you, are simply *pining* for you. There are new puppies, too, Princess, silky, fluffy-ish; you know the sort of thing.'

'There are endless dogs here in all sizes and finishes. I am resolute. I release you from your duty.'

She closed the door.

Many days later, wet through and bedraggled with snow, the same unfortunate equerry rode in melancholy and gloom up the laborious path to the Palace. He was dreading his appointment with the King, knowing his failure would be offset neither by the Buckingham Palace postcard he had sent from London on arrival, nor the two *I visited London* T-shirts (one extra large) that he had brought back in his suitcase.

His failure on this most secret of missions had been absolute, and there was always the Remote Desert lurking at the back of an equerry's mind. He knew of the King's deep reading in historical statecraft, and suspected that for years he had been itching to bellow "Off with his head" to someone or other. Extensive training in diplomatic finesse had refused to come to his aid when he needed it most: he was returning without the Princess. Borisek, his horse, whinnied sympathetically.

The familiar Palace gates came into sight at last. The intricate iron tracery surrounding the royal crest was heavily over-laden with fresh snow. Two sentries, asleep on their feet through long practice despite the temperature, responded to the jingling harness with an automatic salute. The younger heaved at one of the gates until there was just enough room for the horse and rider to squeeze through.

'Just *you*, after all these weeks?'

'Just me. She wouldn't budge.'

'Blast. Bang goes my bet with the under butler. We all had great confidence in you and your profile.'

'She wouldn't listen to a word. Even about the Silukis. Did you get some in?'

'Yes.'

'Well, send them back, or eat them. They won't be needed. Am I completely done for, then?'

'His Majesty has been dead moody this week. Throwing things.'

'God. That does it. Is there no snow at all in the... *Desert*, do you imagine?'

'Not according to the wife. Her brother saw it once. But he would never talk about it.'

There were more sentries at the drawbridge. The old stable-hand who took Borisek off to be rubbed down knew a thing or two about young women, and had been certain there would be no returning Princess. He now stood to win a good deal of money. The equerry patted his horse gratefully as they parted, wondering if they would ever meet again.

'This is it,' he thought miserably, 'the end of my career and all my hopes.'

He stepped reluctantly across the ancient planking into the misleading security of the Palace precincts.

↷ 3 ↶

King Darius woke early in his mountain fastness. He lay by his sleeping wife for a moment, contemplating reluctantly what probably lay ahead of him in another demanding day. Then the King nipped smartly out of bed and hopped over to the window. The floor was beautifully inlaid, but freezing. He parted the heavy drapes and peered out through a small clear patch in the frosted glass.

The usual scene presented itself, that is to say a whitened landscape of uninterrupted snow. In the distance through the clear air could be seen a dark mass, itself topped in white. This was royal forest, and indeed royal forests could be seen from the castle in most directions. The buildings were perched high-up on a comfortably proportioned mountain that wasn't too steep for people returning after a picnic if they knew the route, while it had always managed to look impregnable to marauding enemies. The view inspired the King, as it always did. He felt that his dominions, as dominions should, really stretched as far as the eye could see.

Darius had always tried to be a tolerant monarch. He had, of course, been as strict as tradition demanded with his own children - of whom there were several - when they were young. At the time of this story, however, they were mostly teenagers, and the King was rather relieved to discover when it came to it that he couldn't do much about their behaviour even if he wished to.

The Crown Prince, Julius, for example, was now nineteen. He looked almost exactly like his paternal great-grandfather King Julius the Fourth, a great soldier and statesman in his prime, and long after that. His august figure with long drooping moustaches and fiercely piercing eyes looked out of a blackened portrait in the Dining Hall. When the Crown Prince had been born the King had spotted at once his resemblance to his august ancestor and resolved that his name had to be Julius: the future Julius the Fifth.

Crown Prince Julius was not, however, built in quite the anticipated illustrious-leader mould. He liked early music, non-rhyming poetry, stamp-collecting, mathematics and, from an early age, classifying beetles. He hated noise, swords, helmets, armour, horses and even going outdoors very often. His voice, squeaky in his early years, was now gentle and subdued. He had never been heard to shout. Beetles of many contrasting characteristics thrived with enthusiasm within the Palace and all over the grounds, so his entomological pursuits did not take him, of necessity, far from home. Palace staff had long since learned that a measure of royal approval could be simply earned by finding, and producing, *any beetle at all*.

'Well, the whole situation is just too worrying,' asserted the Queen later that day, seated at her dressing table, studying her eyebrows and coiffure.

The King was across the room, red in the face and bent over his stomach, wrestling with a waistcoat which he had already twice mis-buttoned. As there were twenty-two buttons involved, he was thinking defiantly of his favourite cricket sweater, but it wasn't clean, and he started muttering under his breath, a habit of which his wife always disapproved.

… already twice mis-buttoned.

'It's weeks, now. We simply *cannot* let it go on,' she continued, 'you must do something about it at once. I *mean* it, Darius.'

'And what do you advocate as a practical step at this point, Hephzibah? Last time you came out with this speech I despatched our most promising equerry, and after trying his best he's lost all his confidence and is still not eating properly. Says she wants to be a hermit, or something.'

'Not a hermit, a *recluse*. Although Lord knows the difference. She should be here, selecting a suitable husband out of all these suitors, and producing fat milky grand-Princes and Princesses for us. I'm fed up making excuses to ambassadors that she's "not available at the moment." Some of them have been looking speculatively at the younger two, I notice.'

'So what exactly do you propose? Irena has never been a malleable girl (I'm glad to say), and it has been a long time since I could influence her with a lollipop or a new dolly.'

'Well, that's just the trouble. You have no influence over your own daughter. She should quake at your slightest frown.'

'Like you, you mean?'

'I know you too well for that,' said the Queen after a pause.

'Well, anyway, when do I ever frown? What have I possibly got to frown about? The world's sweetest, cleverest wife, five children, dominions that stretch as far as any eye can manage. My point is, she has never had reason to quake on my account.'

'What about the time she ate several of those rare stamps in one of your Father's albums? You certainly frowned when you had to face the fact that they didn't come out the other end. That was the only time in living memory you actually changed a nappy yourself.'

'Well there was always a chance. You've surely heard of the term 'internal post'?'

'May I remind you that we are about to dine? And why don't you wear something less pretentious? There are no important guests this evening...'

'I'm sorry, Leepy,' said the Queen later that night, disrobing discreetly behind a hand-painted screen that had been in the Palace for generations. 'I consider that we have no option.'

The King was cleaning his teeth, and at these ominous words he paused, clenching the ivory-handled brush apprehensively.

'Yes, dear?' he said through the toothpaste.

'Yes. You'll have to go to London and bring her back *yourself*.'

'Oomph!' said the King. He sat down.

They lay in bed, the Queen just drifting off to sleep.

'I suppose you mean *incognito*?'

'Of course. This is not any kind of state visit. You just *go*. No crown, no sceptre. Just a suitcase and maybe a camera.'

'Hephzibah, I can't face this alone. I could never sleep in a hotel without you. Why don't you just come with me?'

'I'm sorry, Leepy, but I think this is your job. It won't take long. You just go there, get her and come home. It will be much simpler without me. I'd probably get emotional and noisy, or even angry and tactless. You could take one of the older retainers.'

'Oh they're always half asleep nowadays, and none of them speaks usable English. Why don't we just go together, Hephie? You could do some… clothes shopping while I handle Her Ladyship…'

'Mmm. True. But there again, I'd rather go to Paris and shop there.'

'Superb. So would I. When are we going?'

'Oh,' said the Queen, 'I thought I might go for a week or two *by myself* in the spring, to see Cousin Zenobia now she's had the operation …'

'Oh,' said the King, rather crestfallen, 'I see.'

13

∽ 4 ∾

King Darius checked the house number again, and pressed the doorbell with a hesitant fingertip. He moved from one foot to another and told himself he was not at all apprehensive. There was no response but he remembered what the equerry had told him, and after a decent interval he rang again.

Again nothing happened. With a large measure of relief His Majesty stepped back on to the path and looked with disapproval at the neglected flowerbeds in the front garden. Darius closed the garden gate thoughtfully. If Irena wasn't there, she wasn't there. He couldn't stand in the street all day waiting and ringing doorbells. He was a King, not a private detective. She might be away for *days*, anyway. Plan B was called for. And a cup of tea. He had a pocketful of small coins provided by one of the chamberlains out of the china pig in the Hall. This would be a good opportunity to try them out.

There was no café or restaurant to be seen along the main road, so he just turned off to the right, wandering contentedly along. He felt benignly relaxed, unrecognized in one of the world's great capital cities, and blamelessly prevented by circumstances from carrying out his duty. The world was his oyster, and it was now up to him to find a pearl. He thought experimentally of the Queen, back in their bedroom, packing for Paris. Parted from her for the first time in many years, he found he was not missing her at all. On the contrary, he hoped that she would have a really good time with Zenobia, whom he had always loathed. He imagined having to admire modern sculpture in a fashionable gallery with the pair of them and sniggered to himself. Kingly troubles and responsibilities seemed very far away.

Darius came to an interesting-looking junk shop. He peered through the windows. It was shadowy inside and the glass was grimy, but he could see that the shop was crowded with intriguing things. The door wouldn't budge. There was no OPEN or CLOSED sign, but it was now about 11.00 in the morning, and all the surrounding shops were open and about their business. The King rapped imperiously on the door with his walking-stick. When he did it a second time a figure moved in the back room and stood silhouetted in the doorway. The King waved encouragingly through the glass, thinking that he seemed to have spent the whole morning waiting at doors. The figure made its way slowly across the shop floor carrying a large bunch of keys. The door swung open slowly and a white-faced and bent old man was revealed.

'You rang?' he enquired sardonically.

'... *Sire*' added the King under his breath. Despite himself he was taken aback at such a direct address and had to make a great effort to retain his disguise.

'Er, yes, indeed,' he said, 'I was struck from outside by your display, and thought I might possibly find something I wanted here.'

'We're closed,' said the man bluntly.

'I can understand that you must be very *busy* at this time of year.'

'What time of year? This is just any old day in any old week. I was having breakfast. Even antique dealers need to eat occasionally. Not that I can afford to do so as often as nature had in mind.'

'That is just where you're wrong. Today is not any old day. I can tell you in confidence that I am here representing a venerable foreign power and can be privy to substantial purse-strings if circumstances demand. It would undoubtedly be in your interest to permit an inspection of your stock this morning. Of course, if you are too preoccupied with your bowl of cereal, then I'll look elsewhere...'

'Well, I don't mind if you want to take a quick look,' said the man, impressed against his will. It was just possible to believe that his visitor really did have gold coins about his person, although he couldn't say why. 'Come in. I'll be in the back room, finishing up. I don't suppose you are hungry?'

The King shuddered.

'Tell me, my good man, do you ever organise the export of purchases abroad?'

'We used to,' said the man reminiscently, 'at least, my father used to all the time. Millionaires from America, Maharajahs, everybody used to shop here in those days. Yes, I remember when I was a boy the Japanese Ambassador's wife came in one day and bought a huge –...'

'I see,' said the King. He had already calculated out of the corner of his eye that there were more things that needed buying in the shop than he could possibly carry at the airport, with or without his daughter. Perhaps he could send the equerry with a load of old trunks from the cellars to collect the lot. It would probably cheer him up, and that way the Queen wouldn't have to see it all, at least not all at once.

The King put down his walking stick carefully and took off his coat, for fear of catching things on his sleeves. He noticed an intriguing cabinet full of dried spiders, and picked up a grubby-looking old stamp album…

'… And this train set?' asked the King, some time later.

He was hot, and had taken off another layer. The dealer, cottoning on fast, had cleared a space on his large desk, on which his visitor was gradually stockpiling a heap of 'possibles' that varied a good deal in size, age and weight. He was a ferocious bargainer, however.

'A great deal of work …'

'A lot of the paintwork is scratched up,' the King was saying, 'and this rail looks a bit twisted. A great deal of work to put the thing into running order. I wouldn't bother with it, except that it is pleasantly nostalgic to me, and I know my youngest son would be interested. It's different from the other sets at the Pal-'

The dealer opened his desk drawer and pulled out another ledger. He opened it at random and pretended to look up the going price for that kind of train set.

'This looks horribly like rust to me…' said the King, putting the coveted engine down as if no longer interested.

The dealer sighed, and wrote another squiggle on his list with a pencil.

'And this mask, is it Tibetan, or what?' asked the King, some moments later.

He was up a ladder, for the first time in years, energetically investigating dusty framed prints high up above the picture rail. In between the pictures was a terrifying face in red and gold, the lips pulled back over snarling teeth, with protruding, rolling eyes. The effect was rather comic. It struck him that it might make rather a good present for a certain daughter.

৩ 5 ৩

That same daughter, Princess Irena, happened to be many miles away from home that morning. She had left as early as possible in pursuit of sea air, and taken the train to Brighton. At the very moment the King was closing her garden gate behind him she was already stepping carefully in bare feet across the white pebbles that fringed the sea. It was painful, and she tried going faster, but it made no difference. There were few people about. She stood at the edge testing the water and singing to herself.

The Princess had been in England in her new life for about four months. Everything had been new and unexpected. For the first few weeks she had found it difficult to believe that she had really achieved her goal. Now, however, she had found her own feet, and she felt strong and self-reliant.

This was a new feeling. From her earliest years she had been treated in the way that princesses conventionally are, conscious always of encircling duty that had been in place hundreds of years before she was born. She now regretted that she had sent word of her address to the Palace. With each passing day she grew more certain of the wisdom of her decision to escape, and it was tiresome to anticipate that there might be further attempts to lure her home again.

There had been many reasons for her decision to leave. The most compelling was that she had no intention of marrying any of the suitors who were encouraged to present themselves at court. There were always three or four a year, recently even more. She had long since developed a variety of delicately off-putting defence techniques. One was to talk too much to the suitor, nearly all the time and slightly too loudly, never allowing him to bring out the prepared phrases. Another was to talk hardly at all, and then only in a virtually-inaudible whisper, looking down all the time and fiddling with non-existent split ends. A cousin in much the same position had once suggested that a foolproof technique would be to pick one's nose in a leisurely way, but the Princess had never been driven to such an extremity.

There were other beauteous princesses waiting nearby in other lands (although none, need one say, who could rival Irena), and so things had proceeded in this fashion for some while. The Princess, however, had read books and poetry, and the idea lurked at the back of her mind that she might marry for *love*. At the same time, she was quite certain that there was no other reason for which she would ever marry. The trouble was that her two younger sisters were traditionally obliged to wait until she had been signed off before they could come into range for the suitors. This fact weighed heavily on her conscience, for she knew that they were already dreaming of Princes of their own, and resented the way she had dismissed the abundant supply of admirers who made their overtures in the Palace.

Irena had wanted to ask the messenger whether either of her sisters was yet engaged to be married, but kept silent. It would be interesting, she thought, to see whether she would be sent a wedding invitation when the inevitable time came.

a bag of chips.

19

Princess Irena decided on a bag of chips. She adored chips, and they never had any effect on her waistline, which of course was entirely enviable in its proportions. She added far too much salt, and went meandering along the sea-front, peeking through the shop windows looking for something to take home for one of her white walls.

She was pleasantly tired as she plodded up the hill to the station, carrying her package. Fresh air and salt water were a good mixture. She might recommend it to Belshazzar, who undoubtedly needed to get out of the house more often. And she had done lots of drawings in her sketchbook. She found a vacant seat by the window. Lulled by the swaying of the homeward train the Princess fell into a doze. She found herself doing a painting of herself doing another painting, which itself showed a similar scene. The further she peered into the canvas, the more tiny pictures she could make out. She tried to count them, but they got smaller and smaller, and she lost her place. When she looked back to start again, all the Princesses in the pictures did the same. She noticed that they all had untidy hair, blown about by the wind off the sea, unrestrained by disciplinary hair-clips. She woke suddenly, the train echoing through a tunnel. Her own face, pale and thin, danced in the darkened glass. Her hair really was untidy, she thought. What *would* her governess have said?

❧ 6 ❧

Back in his hotel room the King lay on his stomach on the floor happily turning over the pages of his newly-purchased stamp album. There was nothing particularly unusual in it, but it was exciting to check, and he was always on the look-out for specimens that had gone missing on the earlier occasion. He had left the junk shop carrying a cumbersome assortment of parcels, reluctantly leaving behind a wall of boxes sealed with wax and string, and marked with messages in several languages that they were not to be disturbed until called for. The dealer, slightly delirious, had gone rushing out of the back door of the shop to take his wife out to dinner for the first time in many years.

With an effort the King recalled the purpose of his visit. It was now late afternoon and the first day was vanishing, albeit in the most agreeable way. If he were not careful he would have nothing appropriate to record in his diary before going to bed. As he was certain that the Queen would want to inspect the diary on his return, he felt it might be expedient to make another attempt on his daughter's front door. He looked at himself in the bedroom mirror. He looked hot, dishevelled, and uncharacteristically grimy. The contents of the junk shop had been coated with long-standing London dirt, much of it now transferred to the Kingly personage. He sighed again, and courageously turned on the shower.

Just in time he remembered the Tibetan mask for his daughter. He contemplated for a moment the idea of wearing it himself, attached by a piece of elastic from inside his suitcase, while going through the hotel lobby, to see how many guests he could terrify in one go. The temptation was almost too much, but he thought again of Hephzibah and newspaper reporters. He stowed the mask in a sombre carrier bag, and, collecting his London street map, left the room.

The light in the front room was on. The curtains were carelessly drawn, and there was a gap through which a yellowish light shone out to welcome, so it seemed, the weary traveller. The weary traveller stopped at the gate, taken aback. He hadn't really expected his daughter to be at home. In fact, he had been half-hoping that she would conveniently be away for the whole of the stay allowed by his economy return ticket, which was about five days. This unlooked-for appearance was something to be taken slowly, he thought.

After some minutes at the front gate he pushed it open and stepped up the path. Nothing happened. No guard dogs leaped out of the shrubbery. There were no human guards either. Just old milk bottles, parading round the steps. He reached the front door, and rang the bell.

There was a noise from inside the hall, and the hall light went on. The door swung back to reveal the Princess in a long brown overall many sizes too big for her. Her hair was tied up under a scarf. But she still looked like a Princess, and her Father had no difficulty in identifying her as one of his own.

'Hello, Father dear,' said the Princess. 'You look wet through. Come in at once, I'm making cocoa.'

It was true about his being wet, the King discovered. He had walked through the drizzle obliviously, feeling rather refreshed. Now he sneezed.

'Are you not surprised to see me here?'

'No. By no means. Ever since that twerp with the motorbike I have been anticipating a stream of Palace officials. Although I had not expected the Commander-in-Chief at this early phase. I am flattered. I am also immensely glad to see you, Your Majesty.'

The Princess curtsied, kissed her Father three times, and closed the front door behind him.

'Welcome to my own Kingdom. I have the *whole* ground floor, and *half* the garden. The garden is not pretty at the moment, but it will be. Perhaps you could recommend some plants that look nice but need nothing doing to them *at all* once they've been planted?'

'You intend being here some time, then?' asked the King, politely.

'Indefinitely. Quite definitely. Possibly infinitely. Do you drink cocoa?'

'I've only ever encountered it in films, to my knowledge.'

'It's good stuff. Come into the kitchen. I was just trying to fix an old mask to the wall that I picked up today in a junk shop in Brighton. It's rather fine, look.'

Arm-in-arm they moved down the hall and into the brightly-lit kitchen. The King, the product of a lifetime spent within stone walls clad in heavy tapestries and dusty velvet hangings, was much taken with the simple new whiteness that surrounded him. He felt a sudden burst of pride in his runaway daughter, and when he tried to coerce his features into a picture of strict parental disapproval he found he couldn't manage it at all.

The mask in question lay on the table face up, its bulbous eyes gleaming, with two rows of teeth bared in a grimace.

'Great Scott!' said the King. 'Don't tell me you *like* that sort of thing? Where on earth is it from? Are you intending to live with it everyday, having it watching you consume breakfast?'

'Oh, I hardly ever eat breakfast. It's Tibetan, I believe. I'm already very fond of it. I found it all alone under a table in the junkiest shop you could imagine. It was extremely cheap. So I rescued it. I have always liked masks. I thought I might wear it on the bus one day, and see if it resulted in a whole seat to myself.'

'Isn't it a trifle heavy for about-town wear? Mine is.'

'*Yours?*'

'Oh yes. I picked one up myself, only this morning. Absolute snip. Little place round the corner. I expect you know it? Dirt cheap.'

The King had a sneaking feeling that his mask would turn out to be by far the more expensive of the two, but nothing would have persuaded him to reveal the true figure.

'I repeat, *yours?*'

'Surely. I've always liked masks. I've struggled, but there you are. Although the reason I brought this particular one round here this evening was as a small present for you. I hadn't anticipated that the whole place was going to be riddled with Himalayan disguise already.'

'Riddled is I think a distortion of the situation. One solitary mask like this cries out for a companion. They could wink at one another across a crowded room. Could I possibly *see* it?'

'You think I'd dare take it home to the Palace?'

They giggled together, and the Princess carefully removed the parcel from the carrier bag and unwrapped the paper coverings.

The front door banged. The King stood up straight at the cooker, and looked inquisitively at his daughter.

'Oh, that will be our composer. He lives upstairs. He happens to be the only person in Great Britain who knows that I am a Princess. He is appropriately respectful to me now, but I am rather regretful that I told him.'

'Did he believe you, do you think?'

'I think so. But he's very vague. He keeps pencils in his hair. I am sure that if he had a beard he would keep pencils there too,'

'Do you think he will pick up on my own royal identity?'

'Not in that pinny, no. Anyway, keep calm. He only seldom comes down to visit me. Then it is usually to borrow something, or to invite me upstairs to a recital of a new work. Mostly we pass like buses in the street, with a nod.'

'Isn't he terribly noisy?'

'No. He writes inaudible music.'

'Novel approach. I wonder if he is related to the Emperor's new tailor?'

'Not judging by his clothes. I doubt that he has ever had contact with any kind of tailor, visible or otherwise.'

There was a knock at the door. The King started, and looked with longing at the broom cupboard nearby, but his daughter promptly stood in front of it and called out "You may enter" in her most autocratic and leisured tone.

The door opened and a thin spiky person put his head round the door.

'Your Majesty, I wonder if I could trouble you for some milk?'

'Why certainly ...' said the King courteously.

There was an uncertain silence, while the composer looked from one to the other speculatively.

'Er...

... mmm...

er...'

'Come in, Belshazzar, and have some cocoa,' said the Princess hurriedly. 'I don't believe that you've met my Father?'

'Do I bow or just go down on one knee?' asked the composer carefully.

24

He closed the door behind him, and advanced uncertainly into the room. He looked at the King's apron, which was striped blue and white and, truth to tell, needed a wash. It was a tribute to Darius' early training that he was able to give a convincing impersonation of a man fully at ease with his surroundings, although he had probably never before found himself at such a disadvantage.

'Father, this is Belshazzar, the composer who resides upstairs, whom I believe I mentioned to you before. Belshazzar, this is my Father, Darius. The Fourth.'

'Hello,' said the composer.

'There's no need to bow or anything here,' said the King reassuringly.

'I suppose not, in the kitchen,' said Belshazzar. 'You can't rush the preparation of cocoa,' he continued, as one revealing a long-cherished conviction. 'Especially if you've run out of milk as I have. I left half a carton on my window-sill this morning and when I got home it had vanished.'

'Probably a cat burglar,' said the King.

There was another pause.

'Been to Tibet, then?' said the composer, conversationally

25

'Been to Tibet then?' said the composer, conversationally, gesturing at the mask on the table with a pencil that he seemed to have had in his hand already. '*Excellent* cocoa. My compliments to the chef.'

The King smiled modestly. No one could have guessed from his demeanour that it was his first ever experience of cooking anything.

The composer looked thoughtfully at Darius through the steam rising off his cocoa. Could he really be a live king? The problem was roughly the same as that posed by Irena Natasha herself. He had gone along with her story, mostly considering to himself that it was just her fancy. Lately, however, he had begun to wonder if she were not really a Princess after all. What was more, there was something august about the man seated opposite him at the table. His hands looked as if they had done little in the way of hard labour. And his back was conspicuously straight. Perhaps he was a real King after all. If so, perhaps he would be interested in employing a court musician, and might commission works for the launching of a royal barge, or the birth of a new Prince. There could be a whole room of expert musicians poised to perform his music as it fell from his pen…

'Belshazzar, you are spilling your cocoa,' said the Princess.

He finished his drink and rose to leave.

'A pleasure to meet you,' he said politely, and, accepting the Princess's offer of a half-bottle of milk, he made his departure.

↭ 7 ↭

King Darius lay in bed in his hotel room. It was very late indeed. On returning from Irena's flat he had made the mistake of deciding to have a quick look at the train set, which he had been completely unable to leave behind at the dealer's that afternoon.

It had been professionally packed, each item individually wrapped and the whole encased in some bubbly material. The King really just wanted to have a look at his engine, and perhaps wind it up a few times and watch the wheels go round. The smell of the metal parts and the oil when he had half wound it in the shop had brought a flood of memories into his mind, and he wished to relive the experience in privacy, but the items were so well protected that it took him several attempts to identify which was the locomotive. Once so many pieces were half undone it seemed silly not to have a look at the whole train. The old coaches and trucks were much more attractive than they had appeared in the gloomy shop, and he felt doubly excited as they emerged one by one on the counterpane. After that it seemed positively absurd not to try them out on the rail. The box contained a great bundle of track, all tied up together, with one extra piece containing a fork with changeable points, so that a train could be made to go in more than one direction.

Deeply absorbed, the King crawled around on the floor in his dressing-gown, calculating the most extensive area that could be covered by the available resources. He sent the branch-line under the bed, disturbing a good deal of dust in the process. There was an old china chamber-pot shoved a long way back, and by dint of great exertions he was able to send the track right round it to re-emerge out of the darkness, between the legs at the end of the bed, drawing up to the station area and signal box which he planned to locate by the main wardrobe. Once he got everything settled he set the engine and coaches in position and wound up the engine with the key.

Not all the carriage wheels, however, were properly in place. The engine, after years of inaction in a stultifying cardboard box, buzzed frantically in his hand to be off on a run. At that precise moment the telephone rang. The King nearly jumped out of his skin. The engine leapt out of his hand and, freeing itself in a trice from rail and coaches alike, zoomed off under the bed at high speed, coming to rest somewhere out of sight against the far wall. Darius, straining his ears, heard the motor gradually pale to silence as the spring rang down.

The King, sneezing twice, got to the receiver just as the caller disconnected at the other end. He looked at his watch. It was nearly 1.00 am.

'Well, if it's important they'll ring back,' he thought to himself, and tried to tug the bed away from the wall to retrieve his engine. For some inscrutable reason, however, the bed was bolted solidly to the floor.

Darius the Fourth lay on the carpet and looked under the bed again. It was dark as well as dusty, and he could not see the engine at all. A skinny boy chimney-sweep could not have squeezed under that king-size bed, let alone a full-size King in the prime of life. The engine was now several feet away from its new owner. The King looked anxiously round the room for a four-foot pole with a hook at one end, but there didn't seem to be one provided. Next he contemplated telephoning room service, but he couldn't think of a reasonable-sounding request that would produce what he needed. He stamped around the room – quietly – in a state of royal irritation. He helped himself to a fizzy drink from the small fridge and tried to plan calmly.

After half a mile of walking to and fro, Darius had a brainwave: were he to remove the coverings and mattress from the bed he ought to be able to put a hand down between the springs to reach the floor by the wall and rescue his engine. He tugged the bedding out of the way and heaved the mattress on to the floor with a gigantic shove. Minutes later, covered with fluff and dust, the weary King piled his bedding into a heap, and crawled into the middle, depositing the locomotive beside him on his pillow. As he laid it down the spring gave a last twitch of life, and he fell asleep to the gentle whirr of clockwork that echoed particular moments from his most remote boyhood.

. . . the gentle whirr of clockwork

෴ 8 ෴

Over breakfast the following morning King Darius, a little bleary-eyed after his exertions, resolved to tackle his daughter firmly on the question of her return home. His sympathy with her desire for private independence was less pronounced than on the previous day, and he now felt strongly that her place was in the place of her birth, serving her King *and* Queen *and* country. He decided, as he poured an unfamiliar crunchy cereal into his bowl, to take a firm line right from the beginning.

'Get it over right from the start, and then we can spend a nice few days pottering around seeing sights and go home together,' he told himself comfortably.

They were to meet at 10.30 outside the zoo. The Princess had been there to draw several times, and spoke of it with such direct enthusiasm that the King's own interest was kindled. He himself had not visited a zoo since childhood, and his recollection of it was faint beyond a brief ride on the back of a camel that had reminded him of one of his aunts.

The King was early. The Princess, of course, was late. He walked up and down outside the main gate rehearsing some firm diplomatic language for establishing parental and Kingly authority. This was his usual practice when faced with matters of state at home, and he had found that a spot of planning and the preparation of telling phrases often made all the difference. There would be an awkward quarter-of-a-hour, after which his daughter would admit the justice of his views, and agree without further trouble to do her duty. Darius had much confidence in her integrity and upbringing.

'Good *morning*, my dear,' he began, his hands folded behind his back, as the Princess turned the corner and ran delightedly towards her Father. 'You arrive at an opportune moment. I have been thinking. Your Mother and I…'

'Nothing doing,' said the Princess without hesitation. She reached up and kissed her Father's cheek.

'But, my dear young daughter…'

'*But nothing*. Forget it, Your Majesty. I suggest we get this over with right from the start, and then we can spend a nice few days pottering around seeing sights, and then you can go back home and explain everything to Mamma. I am *not* going home with you. And *that* is *that*.'

'But...'

'Father...!'

As a result the following days could pass in light-hearted enjoyment. Neither party alluded again directly to the real reason for the King's visit. Darius acknowledged to himself that, lean on his daughter as he might, there was no real headway to be made in changing her mind, and he decided to give up the battle for the moment. Periodically he suffered a qualm at the thought of having to explain things to the Queen, but most of the time he succeeded in putting that problem altogether out of his mind.

The zoo was a great success with King Darius, leaving him with the conviction that he must found a counterpart at home himself immediately. He had been re-reading the notices that explained about how the breeding of rare species was accomplished by zoos acting in collaboration, and was now talking of a Palace rhino herd and a hot-house full of parrots.

'Julius will want an insect house, of course.'

'Good point. But that won't help with visitor numbers. We will have to consider family discounts, and tickets. Yellow, I think, with an animal motif and the crown at the top. What do you say?'

'Perhaps we could have an *outdoor* pool for our polar bears?'

'Do I take your use of the plurals "we" and "our" to indicate willingness on your part to return with me to take up an appointment as an Assistant Keeper?'

'Not on your life. I was temporarily affected by your enthusiasm. But I couldn't stand the smells on top of all the cultural disadvantages that such a backward move would entail.'

'I see. *Cultural disadvantages. Backward move.* Maybe then it would not be possible for me to coax you into coming home and opening an air-conditioned Art Gallery instead?'

'Very funny. We haven't possibly got enough paintings.'

'Don't be so sure. There is a chamber you've never been in full of dusty old frames leaning against the walls, and I know there are some albums of watercolours somewhere. One of your mother's uncles went on a buying trip before the First War, and came back with *cart-loads* of stuff, I remember. His parents thought they were dreadful. There was talk of a bonfire.'

'*Really?* This does interest me beyond mucking out the family rhinos. Tell me more, Father dear.'

'Oh. I couldn't possibly remember it all. There are so many, whole rooms-full, in fact. Great gold-rimmed oils, and so many *foreign names…,*' said the King airily. 'Anybody interested in that sort of thing would need to come and go through it themselves. Take weeks, probably, if not months…'

The Princess looked at him sceptically, but she knew her Father well, and judged that, allowing for poetic licence and exaggeration, there probably was something unknown to her in the paintings line at home. There were state collections of all sorts of things stored in all sorts of places. She laughed.

The King reacted much the same way on their boat trip down the Thames. He was soon talking of a Royal Yacht. It took concentrated argument on the part of the Princess to remind him that there was scarcely a river large enough in the Kingdom to warrant such an investment, and the rivers that he did possess were iced-over most of the year anyway. Her Father had been in such an expansive mood over lunch that Irena even proposed that they might go to a concert together that evening.

It was something of a family joke that King Darius was utterly tone deaf. It was no mild case. The Queen had more or less forbidden him to sing to the children when they were young after the Court Tutor had taken her aside and warned that the exposure might cause long-term damage. It was not that the King was uninterested in music, but it seldom came about that he listened to any on purpose. The Princess had had the idea that away from his usual life, and uninhibited by critical individuals, her Father might enjoy a concert in a beautiful old room in London. Timing her question carefully she asked him if he would accompany her that evening to a recital. He agreed without hesitation.

She had managed to steer her Father to a small restaurant round the corner from the concert hall. Now they left together, stepping into a fierce bluster that bent them over on the pavement like creaky olive trees. The King clutched his shameful hat, an essential part of his London disguise, and struggled onwards, head down like a polar explorer, while his light-footed daughter clung to his strong arm in comfort, her laughter snatched away with their conversation by the impatient wind.

... by the impatient wind.

∽ 9 ∾

Princess Irena sat in her seat as if hypnotised. She was deeply happy. It was almost dark within the auditorium, a faint light provided by old-fashioned shaded lamps high up near the ceiling, and it was warm. Almost all seats were occupied, and the great chamber was intent upon the lighted, animated figures on the stage.

The first piece of music was for string quintet. The composer must have been a nervous and unhappy individual, she reflected, since the music was subdued and moody even when all the musicians were playing together. She leaned forward, perturbed suddenly by a low but distracting growling that intruded above the delicate melody. At first she thought it must be the cello, but gradually she realised that the sound had nothing to do with the musicians. It was King Darius, fast asleep, snoring gently in a rising and falling rhythm, not quite in time with the music. The Princess felt herself going red, even in the dark. At any minute she expected people to start turning round with disapproving expressions on their faces. Or perhaps the musicians would just stop playing until there was silence again in the auditorium, or the manager himself would come and request the offender to leave. What was she to do?

Urgently, though not painfully, she poked her Father in the ribs. Nothing happened, so she did it again, harder. The King sighed in his sleep, twitched like a horse, and subsided again into a noisy rasp. The poor Princess thought of just running away, but tried pulling on his ear lobe, hard, and pinching it with her nails. This time he woke up with a start, looking around, uncertain where he was. She whispered in her Father's ear. He nodded, and sat up obediently. Irena Natasha relaxed, but some minutes later she saw her Father's head begin to fall forward on his chest again. At least this time he was silent.

The strange music proved popular with the audience. The very minute it came to an end they burst into applause as if by prior arrangement. The explosion of sound roused the King. Drowsily he saw the white sheet of his concert programme slide off his lap and drift to the floor. Leaning forward stiffly to rescue his property, and still only half-awake, he completely miscalculated the movement. He rolled slowly forwards right off his seat on to the floor, landing between the rows of seats in a three-quarters upside-down position on top of his programme.

The speechless Princess heard a whoosh of stifled laughter, and looking across the King's now empty seat she saw a thin, white-faced young man in a worn velvet jacket with both hands pressed over his mouth. Against his better judgment he caught her eye, and immediately all attempts at self-restraint vanished. He burst out laughing so uninhibitedly that the Princess could only do the same. Muffled sounds could be heard from Darius, who was struggling to pull himself up still without being at all certain where he was. The young man pushed a hand under the King's elbow and with help from the Princess succeeded in righting him back into his chair. The King accepted his programme in silence. He shook his head.

'So that's what dethronement feels like,' he whispered to his daughter.

'May I perhaps offer you both a coffee?' asked the young man politely. 'It is the interval now, you know.'

Father and daughter followed him out into the foyer, where the King excused himself and went to wash his hands and face. They joined the end of a snaky queue that wound its way between placards to a small window where refreshments were being dispensed.

'Thank you for rescuing my Father so elegantly,' said the Princess. 'I should have had difficulty managing that without you.'

'Don't mention it,' said the young man gravely. 'It was a pleasure to be of assistance. Does your Father take milk in his coffee?'

He looked very quickly at the Princess when she thought she wouldn't notice.

'You aren't going home immediately, I hope?' he said, without thinking.

'Only my Father,' said the Princess. 'He is on a brief holiday, but has to get back very shortly. It is hard for him to be away from his job for long. It's different for me. I am happy here.'

'You are happy?'

The Princess was about to answer when the King reappeared. They were just up to the window, and moved away with their plastic cups. The young man noticed a sheaf of leaflets advertising a piano recital the following Tuesday, and helped himself to one. While he was thinking of something suitable to say the first bell rang to indicate that the interval was almost over.

'Shall we…?' said the King. He was fully recovered, and seemed to be looking forward to the second half of the programme. He preceded them into the auditorium.

'Would you *possibly* come with me to this recital next Tuesday?' said the young man right near her ear, as he held the door open. He handed her the leaflet encouragingly.

'You'd enjoy the music, I am *certain* and… I… *er*… Meet you here outside at *twenty past seven*?'

The Princess took the leaflet

The Princess took the leaflet and pretended to read it over thoughtfully.

'Sounds like a lovely programme,' she said. 'I should be delighted.'

10

'Let me get this absolutely *clear*, Darius…,' the Queen was saying.

They were standing in the vast Hall, and he was still wearing his greatcoat. She had given him kisses on cheeks, but they hadn't felt like real welcome-back kisses. Her voice was polite, but verging on the icy. The King was just waiting for her to say

'… and you're asking me to believe that you, a *King*, went *all the way to London* and didn't even manage to…'

but he couldn't think of anything to say to prevent it. Darius was extremely tired. The journey had been intolerable, worrying about the parcels from the minute he stepped into his London taxi until he finally climbed down, frozen stiff, from the royal sledge. The footmen were still coming in and putting them down carefully by the marble telephone table. The King watched them out of the corner of his eye.

'And don't think that bringing back a load of presents will make up for it…' said the Queen ominously into his ear.

There was nothing for the Queen

She was growing crosser by the minute. The King half expected her to stamp her foot.

'It's pure *incompetence*. It looks so *feeble*. We'll have to convince everybody that you went to London for another purpose altogether.'

It was at that exact moment that Darius realised that among all his parcels and presents there was nothing at all for the Queen, not even another T-shirt. He went through every box in his mind, but he had done such a good job of shrugging aside the idea of facing her when he got home that he had forgotten to find her a special present. The closest thing to her taste was probably the beautiful Chinese dragon of porcelain that he had found lying under a tarpaulin at the back of the antique shop. It was nearly eight feet tall, with hardly a scratch, and was still there. He'd write at once.

'I *have* got a little surprise for you actually, my dear,' he remarked, 'but it's still in London. I do think you'll approve, though. For a corner of your dressing room…'

The Queen sniffed sceptically, but he had managed to distract her slightly by this statement.

'You are planning on regular trips like this at state expense, then?'

'Regular I doubt. Just the occasional visit to observe the international scene. Trade, high level diplomacy, extradition treaties, one's finger on the pulse…'

'Oh, *really*? I look forward to the official account of your achievements to date.'

'It will remain classified for seventy years, but I can give you the gist, later, in private. Since you are close to the Throne.'

'Do. Well, Leepy, I will admit that I am glad to see you safely returned. It has been a strain acting as Regent. To tell the truth I never really expected you'd bring her ladyship back, anyway. You've always been hopeless with Irena.'

'I'll ignore that unworthy slur. Wait till you try. She wouldn't allow me so much as to broach the subject. So are you going off to Paris, then?'

'No. Zenobia has fallen in love with her surgeon, and they are now in Hawaii, convalescing on the beach. He was going to be removing her stitches at any minute. I thought I'd be rather in the way.'

'But my poor darling, you won't be getting a break at all, will you?' said the King, sympathetically. An idea was taking shape at the back of his mind. 'We'll have to see what we can do about that now, won't we?'

The Queen looked at him suspiciously.

'Well. I'll obviously have to go to London myself and fetch our daughter home, as no one else seems able to accomplish that. That will constitute a sufficient break from my normal routine, I think.'

The King was silent. Time enough, he thought to himself, to discuss all that.

The other children were arriving, the girls first, followed by Julius, carrying Maximilian on his shoulders.

'*Daddy!*' cried Helena and Guinevere in unison.

Julius grinned and waved, nearly dropping his small brother who was leaning outwards and waving the other way at the same time.

The King grinned back and there was a flurry of limbs and embraces and parcels.

≈ 11 ≈

'… and so you see, my dear Sirs, that on one level it must be admitted that my visit to London might not appear to be an unblemished success, in that the Princess Irena Natasha conveyed to me her regretful conviction that for the present (and I am satisfied that it *is* only for the present) she wishes to remain in London, in order to pursue her interest in… er… *Art*…'

There was a murmur among the grey heads in the Audience Chamber. Many of them too had lost money in unwise wagers as to the outcome of the King's trip, and had turned up in full that morning to hear what had really happened.

'… I know that many of you will disapprove of this state of affairs, in as much as it has certain dynastic implications, and perhaps feel that I might more fittingly have insisted on obedience…?'

Again there was a murmur, making it clear that his remarks were being closely followed.

'Well, gentlemen, I have a *plan*…'

'It's rather fortunate that you didn't unpack my portmanteaux,' the Queen was saying at the same time to her Lady-in-Waiting, who was doing her hair. 'It looks as if I'll be needing them anyway.'

The Lady-in-Waiting said nothing, knowing from much experience that this was certain to be the wisest policy.

. . . the wisest policy.

ॐ 12 ॐ

The Princess walked steadily towards the concert hall. She had thought several times over the last few days about going to meet her young man. She wasn't at all nervous or apprehensive. On the contrary, she felt excited inside and calm outside.

He was there outside the building waiting for her, but not looking at all as she expected, nor was he holding flowers or chocolates. He seemed uncharacteristically anxious, and ran up to her the minute he saw her.

'He's *ill*. The pianist. There's no concert today. It's all been *cancelled*. I've brought you here under false pretences.'

... false pretences.

'Calmly. It is scarcely your fault. Perhaps you could sing to me instead?'

'You would leave.'

'Is the piano more your forte, then?'

'No. I cannot play with both hands and breathe at the same time. Can you? Could you bear to come for a walk with me instead, with no musical accompaniment?'

'Of course I can play the piano. Of course I could bear to go for a walk with you.'

The Princess tucked her arm in his, and they turned away from the door with its notice saying CONCERT CANCELLED, and strolled together up the street. The Princess noticed that although his legs were a good deal longer than her own their strides were about equal length.

'Your name is Irenka?'

'Irena Natasha. The –ka ending is an affectionate diminutive. You must then have heard my Father addressing me?'

'Indeed. How is he? What am I to call you, then?'

'He is well. Back in harness, I should imagine. You *could* call me Irenka, I think, since you have started out that way, and you are certainly taller than I. What is your own name, incidentally?'

'Bartholomew.'

'I see. Do you have brothers and sisters, Bartholomew?'

'Several of each. Any number. I am the youngest, apparently the most spoilt, and the least successful commercially.'

'I am taken aback to hear you judge yourself by such a criterion.'

'I am quoting from my elders and betters. I am trying to follow a path with which they are not in sympathy. I paint. I have a garret that I call my own. I know how to starve.'

'I note that. What do they call you?'

She had spoken without hesitation. *He's a painter*, she told herself. *Of all things…* Her heart lurched peculiarly, just for a second. He was answering her.

'They avoid use of my name wherever possible, and refer to me by low epithets. My governess called me Bartholomew. What did your governess call you?'

'Oh, she was never allowed to address me so directly.'

'I think having a lot of brothers and sisters is a good arrangement, but it can be top heavy if you are at the bottom.'

'That is an experience I have never known. I am myself the oldest of five, but my own small brother seems to have resisted any attempts at flattening. I shall call you Bartholomew.'

'I should be happy if you were to do so. This doesn't mean that you will also be giving me homework?'

'It's not inconceivable.'

They wandered on without paying much attention to their whereabouts.

'Let's go down to the river,' said Bartholomew absently.

Actually, at that moment, he wasn't quite sure where the river was, but reckoned they were bound to bump into it sooner or later. All he really wanted to do was continue walking with her.

'Tell me, Bartholomew, do you like junk shops?'

'Curious that you should ask,' came the reply, 'I adore them but whenever I find one it *always seems to be shut.*'

↶ 13 ↷

It happened then that a small embassy from distant parts which had been expected for at least a fortnight finally arrived - without warning or trumpets - at the Palace. It transpired that they had got themselves grievously lost, only to discover that no one in the party had a compass in his luggage. They were all, understandably, conspicuously undernourished.

The Principal Chamberlain was a resourceful man, and hot water and rooms were always ready for ambassadors, suitors or adventuresome travelling salesmen. The small party was ushered upstairs to one of the guest wings with the minimum of fuss. There might have been a slight problem in that a similar party was due to arrive from almost the opposite direction at any moment. The Chamberlain was not worried: they might get lost, too. Would-be visitors often did.

'Leepy, I want your proper attention. I am prepared to go to London, in fact I've packed already, but I want to ask you something before I make any serious plans. Do we or do we not wish to start marrying off our other daughters?'

'Why, what has happened? I've been a bit preoccupied with pacifying the Elders this week. A rumpus about some busybody fiddling about with their seats in Council. Has something happened about the girls?'

'That busybody was I. Those seats quite incontrovertibly need re-covering. Anyway, I have an idea that the thinner one at dinner yesterday rather fancies Guinevere. The Chamberlain gave me all the details this evening on this sheet of paper. It's a very old family, and, more important, he is an only son. There is a good deal of solid family worth behind that boy. Several famous ancestors. Somebody invented a hot-air balloon, or something. Ask Julius, he's bound to know. Actually, now I mention it we could do a lot worse than consult Julius about delicate state matters of this kind. He may have to succeed you one day, after all.'

'Isn't the thinner one the chap who got lost? He must be an awful bonehead to arrive two weeks late for dinner.'

'I gather he was reading a three-volume novel with the curtains shut against the draught, and just left the navigation to his Captain of Horse. It was he who brought them in, apparently, using a stick in the wind and an empty yoghurt pot.'

'Bit of a clever clogs, you mean? Wouldn't he be rather tiresome over charades at Christmas?'

'Leepy, do concentrate. We must decide about the future life of our daughters on the basis of important factors.'

'Well, you take charades pretty seriously when it comes to it.'

'Leepy, I'm tired…'

'What about the *fat* one? Any interest in young Helena? Be a lot cheaper to pull off a double wedding.'

'Darius, I am going to sleep. We'll talk about it tomorrow. You shouldn't have eaten so many hot peppers at dinner. It's unsettled your psychology.'

'I like the idea of all our girls marrying whomever they fall in *love* with. I want them to be *happy*.'

So said the King rebelliously, under his breath, once he saw that his wife was asleep. He knew only too well that this sentiment was a minority view at the highest level in the land. Nevertheless, he thought to himself, *you never know*, Your Majesty, you just *never know…*

Darius recalled over breakfast the following morning that he was committed that week to visit the state ice-hockey team in the south, who had been training up for a long time for international competition and now really needed some encouragement. They all happened to be quite unaware that their King despised sports of any kind, his loathing covering anything more energetic than the tossing of an occasional snowball. It was for this reason that the Queen was archly incredulous when the Herald mentioned to her that the King would be away for three or four days on a Royal Inspection, and he felt it necessary to produce the court diary and show her the entry.

'But Vanya,' said the Queen in reasonable tones, 'His Majesty *hates* ice hockey. I've known him leave the room when that sort of activity is even mentioned on the radio.'

'Indeed, Your Majesty,' said the Herald guardedly, 'but I gather that certain very poignant letters were received, and His Majesty was moved to feel a certain sympathy, to the point of making a symbolic gesture at this time.'

... a symbolic gesture ...

'Travelling across the icy wastes in his royal person? He'll probably catch a lethal consumption out there at this time of year,' she continued.

'I shall undertake to ensure that His Majesty is suitably bundled up, Your Majesty.'

'I wonder what the reaction would be if I evinced a sudden interest in encouraging national netball?'

'Well, Ma'am, I believe there are certain netball teams within our borders for whom an indication of royal patronage would be an immense boon. My niece tells me –

'Steady on, Vanya. I was merely thinking aloud. Don't start planning anything.'

'No, Ma'am.'

Later that morning the King was to be found leaning over the billiard table in the basement knocking a few meditative balls about on his own. The same Herald was standing under the scoreboard at the far end watching his lord and master in respectful silence, with a small piece of French chalk at the ready. The King attempted an unusual manoeuvre with the cue that drove a ball straight over the edge of the table on to the wooden floor with a bang. Vanya stooped to retrieve the missile.

'What did she say, Vanya? I dare say she was surprised?'

'She was, Sire. Sceptical, if anything. She gave me to understand that she found your active interest in promoting ice hockey to be something she had not allowed for.'

'Well I'll tell you something, Vanya. A King can get stuck in a rut. Or fall prey to a closed mind. These over-athletic types out in the far reaches are also my loyal subjects, and I consider that they are putting on an impressive show. Somebody in a country like ours has to be happy batting things around on the ice, after all, there's so much of the stuff lying about. It would be absurd if some tropical blighters ran off with the title wouldn't it? So, I see their endeavours as a form of patriotism. Also, between you and me there's an old friend of mine who lives down there with a fantastic collection of stuff that I haven't seen in ages. Could you pack me an overnight bag or two? I think I'll take you, that unfortunate equerry, and a couple of the lads for the sledge. You can get away?'

'Well, Sire, there are the various parties in residence, but the chamberlain has everything in hand. He was thinking of taking steps to dislodge the… er… heavier party.'

'Would that be the tame mice, or the apparition thing?'

'We thought in this case the ghost would have more dignity. The trouble with the mice is that it gives people the idea that the Palace is unhygienic, and the staff always take hoovering and loose crumbs very seriously, as you know.'

'Indeed, Vanya. Incidentally, is there anybody on the staff who knows the rules of ice hockey, or could lend me a book on the subject? It would be helpful to have some idea of how you *tell the winner…*'

14

'I think I should like to go *paddling*,' announced the Princess.

Bartholomew was feeling rather pleased with himself that he had managed to locate the River Thames this time, and was enjoying looking at the Princess's face whenever the wind blew her hair out of the way. He thought she was utterly beautiful, but wasn't quite sure whether he could mention it. She was, it was quite obvious, unlike any other person he had encountered. He thought she probably knew that she was beautiful, and supposed that many people must have told her so, but he did doubt that anybody else had ever understood as he did quite how beautiful she was. There were many things about her that pointed to a world quite different from his own behind her, about which he knew nothing, but at the same time she seemed to him in every way utterly familiar.

'I don't quite see how one gets down to the water from here,' the Princess was saying.

Bartholomew looked over the wall. The water, black and oily, was far below the parapet, and there was no possible access unless you were a seagull.

'I think we must defer paddling. This is water with complications.'

'If I give up the idea would you buy me an ice-cream?'

'Since it's a really cold day, you mean? Of course I will. Why don't we go and feed the pigeons in Trafalgar Square? Like proper tourists.'

They strolled on. It was not what the Princess would have described in any way as a cold day.

'I say, Bartholomew, have you… travelled much in your life so far?'

'France, Europe, a few places in America. Brighton. Hackney.'

'I see. Have you been anywhere truly freezing?'

'My flat.'

'Anything more adventurous?'

'America. If you breathed in outdoors during January in Chicago the hairs inside your nose went stiff.'

Bartholomew looked over the wall.

'I see. You have never been, say, to the *North* Pole? Or the *South* Pole?'

'Mmm. Let me think. No. I always get off the train in time. Should I have done one of them by now, do you think?'

'No, no. Not at all. What about … Siberia?'

'Well, the judge let me off with a warning. Mind you, I did go to *Birmingham* once.'

'Oh, that's all right then.'

'Good. While we're on this sort of subject, Irenka, I wanted to check with you as to whether by chance you happen to have put in a twelve month vacation on Easter Island?'

She grinned at him and shook her head firmly. The Princess said nothing. It was definitely not yet time, she thought, to explain to her companion the reason for her questions.

↻ 15 ↻

The King's party had been on the road for many hours, and now that it was growing dark he was beginning to regret the impulse that had led him to undertake the trip. Arrangements had been made at the last minute for an overnight stop at an ancient inn. It was snowing heavily, and the party at the back on the great sledge were in low spirits. The Herald passed a small flask to his Sovereign. The sovereign passed it back shortly after, with an appreciative wink.

One driver shouted out something. The Herald translated.

'We are arrived, Sire, I believe.'

'So we are. Thank Providence.'

They had reached the outskirts of a small village. The snow was churned up and muddy through the main street where horses, carts and sledges had passed during the day. Cottage windows shone out under low thatching, and grey smoke billowed from every chimney. The Herald felt homesick for his grandmother's village. Darius felt much more cheerful, and hungry.

'There's the inn.'

They tumbled, stiff, to the ground, and the boys drove the sledge round to the stabling at the rear. It was bright and very warm inside.

'*Brilliant*. I *told* you he'd come. Here's the King himself,' said the innkeeper to his wife.

The innkeeper's wife blushed, and reached behind her automatically for a key, sliding the guest book across the desk uncertainly.

'Quite right,' said the King. 'Quite right. Careful bookkeeping. Highly commendable. Now, what room number am I? Damn, where's my pen? I say, can you lend me something to write with? How many are we, Herald…?'

Shortly after the King rose sleepily out of the hottest bath that he could coax from the plumbing, and stood on the mat wrapped in his towel. It was spotlessly clean, and pleasingly dissimilar to

51

his linen at home. Darius inspected himself in the steamy mirror wrapped in vibrant stripes and ducks. He thought he made rather a Kingly figure. He re-enveloped himself in toga-like form and drew a face in the glass.

There was a very small knock at the door.

'Your tray will arrive in ten minutes, Sire,' said a squeaky voice through the keyhole. The King bent down to look through. He saw part of a small boy with very neatly combed hair just the other side of the door.

'Thank you,' said Darius stoutly.

The small boy bowed, even though he had no idea that the King could be watching him. Darius felt deeply gratified. He put on his royal dressing-gown and brushed his own hair. He was looking forward to his supper. He was quite ravenous, in a Kingly way.

There came another, slightly louder knock.

The smell was irresistible.

'Enter,' said Darius. Then it struck him that it might be awkward for someone outside to open the door if they were holding what he hoped would be a groaning tray. He opened the door himself. There were other small and very clean-looking children outside. A particularly diminutive girl carried a bunch of flowers. She curtsied. Two boys carried trays laden with tureens and napkins and shiny cutlery. The smell was irresistible.

'I say, that looks wonderful. Well done!' said the King. He took the tray from the first boy and put it on the table, then collected the second. He picked up a napkin thoughtfully.

'Father-said-the-wine-will-be-along-in-a-minute-Your-Majesty,' said the larger of the two boys.

They bowed in unison and left the room walking backwards, bumping into one another, but managing to squeeze simultaneously through the door into the hallway. Their sister was left behind. She turned round and ran after them.

'Incidentally, have you chaps got a train set?' asked the King through the doorway.

'Yeh, but the spring's gone in the green engine,' said the smaller boy.

'Catastrophic,' said the King. 'I know the feeling. Bring it to me in the morning and I'll see what I can do.'

An older boy with a white cloth over his arm appeared with a silver bucket.

'By Jove,' said Darius, 'this is what I call service. You chaps will have to come and work at the Palace.'

He closed the door gently, tucked in his napkin, and turned on the radio. He always liked to listen to radio plays when dining, and it was but seldom these days that he had the chance to do so.

Queen Hephzibah, meanwhile, abandoned at headquarters, was extremely touchy, and refused to dine again with her guests, calling for deliveries to her rooms. The King's abrupt disappearance on such a preposterous mission irritated her, all the more so in that her disapproval had failed to produce a deterrent effect. To compound the matter he had gone off without further conversation at all about daughters and the marrying business, and that irritated the Queen even more. She had for years resented the way he left so many business decisions to her, not realising that in his eyes there was often, as in the present case, no decision to be made.

The King considered that his wife's impatience to marry off her offspring was slightly indecent, and wanted to leave the matter entirely in the hands of nature. On top of that, he privately favoured the idea of reviving challenges for would-be bridegrooms. Darius felt that if some young prince or other suitor came forward to ask for the hand of one of his daughters, he should be allowed to set them an impossible task, just to establish their credentials. Occasionally at dinner, while being outwardly polite to an unwanted guest, he would dream up a diabolical challenge in the old-fashioned vein.

The Queen's views were profoundly different. In her eyes daughters were a liability, and the sooner they were settled into diplomatically and sociably sound marriages the better. Her chances now of influencing the wilful Irena were minimal, and she was worried that the two younger girls might follow her example. In this fear she was in part mistaken, since both Helena and Guinevere were themselves preoccupied with the idea of securing a fiancé, although it must be admitted that their preferred types of candidate might not have scored high on their Mother's lists.

The problem that tormented the Queen now was whether or not they should ignore protocol and begin work on marrying off their second daughter, Helena, before Irena was safely married. The steady influx of suitors, even if arriving with Irena in mind, could not be let go to waste.

16

There was a plump envelope with a familiar stamp waiting at home for the Princess. She opened it carefully. There were four letters at once:

To: *Irena Natasha*
From the desk of: *Daddy, or me actually*

Dearest Reen,

Things are really hotting up here. Mother is still furious with you and horribly irritable with us. Now the weather is improving she is talking about going to London to fetch you home so <u>be warned</u>. Me and Guinea are really fed up here, but our chances of escape now are worse than those of a cat in a violin factory, as Vanya would say. If she had any idea how restless we were she'd lock us up in one of the Towers. You wouldn't believe the idiots that are here visiting at the moment. One is tall and skinny and the other is a total <u>butterball</u>. And their conversation! Mother thinks we have to be nice to them in case they want to marry us. I'd rather die and so would Guinea. Really she's got no idea what we're really like. She bullies everyone. Poor Dad fled to some mad escapade out in the country just for a few days peace and quiet. I worried what will happen if she goes to London. Maybe you should go away on a holiday. If I find out in time I'll tell you the dates.

Your loving sister,
Helenka x x x x x

P.S. She's got plans for you that you <u>won't</u> like. I've heard her discussing it with Daddy. If I were you I'd go to Australia and start a sheep farm under a false name.

P.P.S. Have you bought any nice clothes in London?

Dear Irena Natasha,

I'm sorry to have to say this but I think you are being extremely selfish staying on in London when you are needed here to restore peace in the family. Mother will never be tolerable while you are absent like this, although I for one do not see why life cannot go on as usual. I don't know whether you realise this, but she keeps muttering about "lost chances" every time we have a male visitor under ninety and you're not here. Meanwhile we have to suffer her filthy temper. Helena and I want to go to Paris and New York and we'll never have the chance until you come home and behave dutifully. I think you have had long enough.

Your loving sister,
Guinevere x x x

Darling Princess, Mamma is on the warpath.
I recommend a trip to Scotland with no forwarding address.
In haste and death-defying secrecy,
Your loving Father and Rex
Dad

Dearest Irenka:-

How <u>sensible</u> of you to be away at this time, since Her Majesty is excelling all past performances. I am seriously contemplating lowering myself by knotted sheets on to a waiting horse beneath my window and coming over there to join you. I need to visit the Natural History Museum as I have a beetle to show one of the curators. I don't remember to have encountered it listed in any of the standard publications. Would you like me to send you a photograph of it? Have you found any good beetles over there?

Your entirely sympathetic and loving brother,
JULIUS
Crown Prince etc. etc.

The Princess read her letters through one by one, twice. It was a relief that her mother hadn't written too. She felt partly encouraged and partly guilty. She finished her coffee and turned on the radio.

'… gale force winds will be sweeping across the south of the country over the next twenty-four hours…'

'That sounds like fun,' said the Princess out loud. It crackled in response.

She decided it was time to speak to Bartholomew. There was a shared telephone in the hall of his house, but for her it was a matter of finding a working public call box with nobody using it. She stepped out of the front door to find that the storm was already at work in her own street. It was no easy matter to walk. Her clothes flapped about madly like fledgling wings, and the only way for her to make progress was to struggle, bent over like an old woman, clawing her way up the street step by step. Things flew by, newspapers, milk cartons and other more alarming missiles.

Gasping she reached the kiosk and struggled round the side to find the door. It took most of her strength to open it. The door snapped to sharply behind her and she was in sudden silence after the roar of the street. Irena picked up the phone and put the receiver to her ear, listening to the purr. She had insufficient strength to dial the number. A man walked past outside and stared at her rudely through the window. She spoke briefly into the receiver as if participating in a conversation, and then paused as if listening to the reply. The receiver suddenly came to with a click as if realising that it was not involved in a real conversation at all. The Princess replaced the leaden receiver. She stood weakly against the wall staring into the distance. Then, of a sudden, she saw Bartholomew in the street outside the phone box, walking in the direction of her house. She cried out and banged on the glass, but in the clamour he didn't hear her. Everything around her grew dim and confusing, and she felt herself slide to the floor.

Her great agitation somehow communicated itself to Bartholomew. For a reason he couldn't explain he promptly turned right round and out of the corner of his eye saw a girl slumped against the glass panels. It was only when he had wrenched open the door that he recognised who she was.

He recognised who she was

People began to collect round them, even though just before the pavement had been empty. He knelt by the Princess and gently raised her to a sitting position. She looked at him. She was very white.

'Is she all right?'
'What happened?'
'Poor dear.'
'It's OK,' said Bartholomew. 'I think it must have been too stuffy inside the phone box.'
'Plenty of fresh air out here,' said somebody else. Several people were holding the door open, and the wind breezed in and out of the confined space, bringing dusty leaves with it.

The Princess smiled up at Bartholomew.
'Are you ready to stand up?' he asked. 'I was looking for your house. Just wanting to drop in for a minute.'
'It looks as if I am the one to do the dropping,' said the Princess. She stood up carefully. 'Without my parachute.'
'She's all right...' went the word.
'Breathe in deeply,' said someone.
'No need for an ambulance, then?'
'Have you had any breakfast, dear?'
'Indeed, good question; have you...?' asked Bartholomew.
'Just some coffee,' admitted the Princess.
'Naughty girl,' said Bartholomew. 'We'll have to do something about that.'

He put his arm around her and she stepped on to the pavement. There was an abrupt lull in the wind. The passers-by began to disperse. They set off like wounded soldiers down the street in the direction of Irena Natasha's house.

'I apologise for not bringing a white horse to the rescue,' said Bartholomew, 'but he's with the farrier. I could give you a piggy-back instead?'

'The exercise will do me good. Please do not concern yourself. I came out of the house to telephone you. I have no idea why the effect was so dramatic. I have made successful telephone calls before, on my own two feet.'

'We must consider alternatives.'

'Bartholomew, may I take this opportunity of inviting you to my house for a spot of breakfast? We are fast approaching the right address, as you know. I am concentrating myself on the idea of toast and honey.'

'Unbeatable scheme. But thickly spread, I think, as recommended by high authority.'

'I should not care to consider any other type.'

They reached the house. The Princess found her door key. Bartholomew stepped back as she unlocked the door.

'Welcome, Bartholomew. I went out in order to invite you for toast and honey, and here you are.'

Bartholomew's heart was racing excruciatingly and he could hardly breathe. He followed the Princess into the hallway and closed the front door behind him. A half-light came through glass panels in the door which were decorated with grey etched flowers in vases. The Princess stood in the shadowy hall and they looked at one another.

'Welcome, Bartholomew,' she repeated.

17

There were, by this time, many objects collected in Irena's kitchen, not all of which by any means were meant for cooking. She had found several other pictures, lots of cookbooks, and a whole row of battered teapots, while a set of old weights apparently sufficient for weighing a prize-fighter was piled in a corner. None of her own drawings was out, however. Her very first purchase, the empty picture frame, still hung on its nail over the kitchen table. Bartholomew looked at it.

'Take off your jacket,' said the Princess, filling the kettle. 'I shall slice an excessive quantity of bread and start proceedings.'

Bartholomew nodded. He felt heavy in his limbs, as if in a dream. He opened a cupboard that seemed likely to contain cups and saucers, but it was full of a hundred other things, none for eating or drinking. He pulled out a straw hat. The Princess laughed.

'Sit down, Bartholomew. Leave this to me.'

After breakfast Irena excused herself for a moment and left the room. Bartholomew waited until she was out of earshot, and leaped to his feet, tugging a large black pencil out of his upper jacket pocket. With a minimum of swift lines he drew a sketch of the Princess on the white wall inside the picture frame. He captured with a touch the face about which he had thought so much, and he was just adding some unkempt hair and a headband when he heard her footfall and returned hurriedly to his seat. He picked up the local paper, and was casually browsing through the advertisements when she came back into the room.

'Would you care to buy an iguana, Irenka?' he asked. 'There's one for sale here. Seems quite reasonable. I'm sure you must have a suitable cage secreted somewhere in that cupboard.'

'I know my Father hankers after a parrot. Would an iguana do instead, do you think?'

The face about which he had thought so much

'As a species they favour reticence. Tell me, Irena Natasha, do you feel better now we have demolished all the toast in the house?'

'I do. I could accommodate one further cup of tea, I think. But not that amusing kind with milk.'

'Pray allow me…'

↝ 18 ↜

The Queen knocked commandingly on the outer door of Julius's rooms, and, not quite waiting for an answer, marched straight in anyway. Her son was lying on the floor, waving one leg in the air and writing in the margin of an encyclopaedia.

'Julius. It is a beautiful day outside. I think you need some mountainous oxygen. Come for a walk in the grounds with me, please. I want to talk to you.'

'Oh,' said Julius.

The Crown Prince wasn't keen on proposals involving walks or talks, but he clambered to his feet and reported obligingly for duty. He was tall and bony and rather pale, and seemed to have grown since the Queen had last looked at him so closely.

'I'll go and find my hard outer protective layer,' he said.

They left by a side door, their feet crunching on the gravel.

'Your Father and I...' said the Queen.

'Yes, Mother dear...?'

'... feel that it is high time you began to shoulder some state responsibilities. One day, let us hope in the very distant future, you will be King yourself, Julius, and we might not be quite here to advise you. Statecraft is complex and demanding, and it seems to us that your studies so far might not have entirely equipped you in the way you will need.'

'I don't know about that. There are many lessons to be learned from entomology. If this Palace showed a greater similarity to an ant colony, for example, things would proceed more efficiently and more economically.'

'Well, even if we follow your suggestion and pretend to be ants all day long, you will still need a Queen, won't you?'

'You know how Queen ants behave at home?'

'Don't be awkward, Julius. You need to think seriously about these things. You can't be a King on your own. How would you manage at dinner parties? How would you produce an heir, now we're on the subject?'

'Mother dear, we are not on that subject. And it is too much to ask me to worry about producing a successor when I am still only a bachelor Crown Prince. Anyway, I want to go to Paris. I want to study entomology properly. With a professor in a white coat. And benches. And microscopes.'

'Julius, you *have* a microscope. A corker. It magnifies like anything. I can still remember that atrocious thing you made me look at when we gave it to you for your birthday.'

'Just a death's head hawk moth. And it is a lovely microscope. I use it every day. I just want to go and work with a few other people interested in the same field.'

'You seriously maintain that there are other people interested in these things?'

'Oh yes. There is a Professor in Paris who said that I could go and work in his laboratory for a year. He needs an assistant.'

'Does he know who you are?'

'Not in detail. I wrote to him saying that I was an enthusiastic amateur rather on the fringe of things needing some practical experience and training.'

'What do you mean on the fringe of things? I shouldn't let your Father hear such talk.'

'I was speaking purely entomologically.'

'You know that the girls want to go off, now, and that Irena refuses to come back at all. At this rate it will just be your Father and the baby to keep me company at Sunday lunch.'

'I should certainly come back. I wish to put our country more emphatically on the entomological map. You see, Mother, I need a teacher to help me prepare for my real work. Once I'm King I'll never have the chance to do this. I am trying to look ahead, in stately fashion.'

'You are telling me that you are planning on continuing in this mode even when you are on the throne? Ruling, as it were, on hands and knees, big game hunting under the sofa?'

'Absolutely. I shall hold an annual conference in the Palace and invite the world's great entomologists for discussions. There aren't so many. We could put them up in the guest wing. These are people who know what the word wing means.'

'Julius, I think I need to sit down. I have always considered this a boyish phase out of which you would, one day, grow in spurts.'

'Also, this Professor has a beautiful daughter. She speaks many languages, and has helped her Father since childhood classifying specimens and mounting them for study. She could, I thought, help me with the State National Insect Museum.'

'I don't recall noticing this State National Insect Museum in any of the guide-books, Julius. And how do you know she's beautiful, may I ask?'

'Oh, she happened to be in one or two photographs that the professor sent me in a letter. She was in the background preparing slides. She has really exquisite hands. I wrote and asked him who she was. Her name is Francesca. We've been corresponding.'

Her name is Francesca

'Oh, you have. Julius, dear, let's go back now. I wish to speak with your Father.'

'He's down in the basement repairing someone's clockwork

engine.'

'So I heard. Thank goodness he was there on hand… Sometimes I feel I'm the only adult in the whole Palace.'

'Well it takes two pairs of hands, one to hold the engine, the other to replace the spring. Dad was going to try it on his own, but the clock man came in at just that moment to wind the grandfathers in the audience chamber and invited him down to his workshop where he has a particularly convenient set of pliers.'

'Oh, don't misunderstand me, Julius. Such crucial matters must always take precedence. Forget the balance of payments. Gloss over civil unrest or failure in the vineyards. Apparently the smart shiny engine belongs to some children he met last week in the country, and we can't have the little drivers disappointed now, can we?'

The Queen glowered savagely, and they went back into the Palace in silence.

∽ 19 ∽

To: H.:
From: D.: c/o the Clocksmith's Room, the Basement

Dear Hieronymus [wrote the King in rather a scrawl, later that afternoon], *what a pleasure to see you again, not to mention your collection. We really must manage to meet up more frequently, and since you are more flexible than I these days (in more ways than one), you must come here within these walls. There will soon be my new consignment arriving from London. I want you to come and admire it. I have been thinking a great deal about our various accumulations of oddities, and have a possible scheme brewing at the back of my mind. Her Majesty is a little fatiguing at the moment, and rebellion is brewing in re the offspring. Mind you, if she does go to London we could get the big train set out in the basement here, and even leave it out for a few days. What do you say? You could bring some of yours over…*

On another subject, I forgot to ask you about your own boys. The Queen was very sarcastic when she asked for family news of you and I realised I had totally forgotten to enquire.

Come here soon.
That's an order
Your old friend
Darius R.:

To: Irena Natasha
From: Dad c/o the Clocksmith's Room, the Basement

Dearest Irenka,

Just me again. I thought I'd fill you in on a sudden turn taken by my career. I have been offered the job of Captain of the girl's national hockey team in the low country, as the direct result of cheering myself hoarse from the lines in a ferocious match against a neighbouring club last week. Once Vanya had explained the rules to me I really enjoyed it, and had a firm grasp most of the time as to which was our side. Most fortunately we won, and everybody said it was because I was there. I still cannot quite understand what prompts people to hit things with sticks, but there you are. Tomorrow the Olympics. After we managed to escape Vanya drove me to old Hiero's estate where I had a wonderful couple of illicit days pottering about in his cabinets. He is supposed to be from one of those old and impoverished families that cannot even afford to run the heating, but he has managed to amass a wonderful mixture of things over the last forty years. Quite a lot in your line, but not a Tibetan mask to be seen.

Now, things are a bit hairy chez nous, and you are in deadly peril of a short term State Visit of a certain type. I am going to speak plainly to your Mother one of these days since I cannot find it within me to endorse her rigid views about your various futures. Between you and me I intend to get over to London again before too long, so start booking some concerts.

I understand your reluctance to discuss certain things last time, but now I need your help, and I think I am going to have to ask you something about your own long-term plans. Perhaps you could try and decide whether you are a Princess who will ever come home? More, perhaps, later. I want to get this in the post. Speak soon.

As ever, your especially tolerant but today uneasy Father.
Dad x x x
P.S. Do you have a telephone number over there yet?

a wonderful mixture of things ...

20

'I have decided to seize control of this family once and for all,' stated the Queen flatly. They were preparing for bed.

She had filled her husband in on what she had learned from Julius that afternoon, and she was now furious all over again because her disclosures produced no real effect on him. Darius took a deep breath, slowly, and knotted the string of his pyjama trousers.

'I really don't see there is any need, Hephzibah. They are just young people who need to stretch themselves and see something of the world outside this oversized igloo.'

'That is just the point, Darius. They are NOT "just young people." They have special responsibilities. They have a *heritage* behind them, and *duty* before them, especially Julius. Do you want to see this nation turning into a colony of beetle-bottlers? If we leave it to him the papers will only be allowed to report on discoveries down a microscope. Two-legged life forms here will become a minority issue.'

'I think we might concede without blustering that his interest is located in the lower orders of a Kingdom quite different to ours. But if he is truly a scientist, should he not be encouraged to follow his natural inclinations? I have no intention of popping off tomorrow, Hephzibah. Unless something unexpected happens he ought to have time now to pursue his scientific career for a few years in peace.'

'Darius, he wants to work in some laboratory in Paris, hobnobbing with flies and bugs, wearing his white coat all day and washing up test tubes. In its place learning is all very well and good, but in my opinion he would do a great deal better studying international finance or the twentieth-century history of smaller countries.'

'I'm not so sure. I did some of those Brush-Up-Your-Statesmanship classes myself before we were married, if you remember. Waste of time. Some know-it-all without a crown of his own yakking on for hours on end. Anyway, maybe the populus would be impressed to have a King who was also a professor. Which title comes first, do you know?'

'Leepy, your inability to stick to a serious point could be celebrated in ballads. That boy will have to be King one day, in a world that is becoming ever less easy to live in, and all his free time now should be put to use in preparing him for that task.'

'I have to say, Hephzibah that I don't agree with you about this at all. Better that he should go to Paris for a year or two and try on his white coat. Let him *enjoy* life before the millstone drops on him. He'll have all the advisors he needs, PhD's and what-not, in Council.'

'Next thing he'll probably want to marry the daughter. He's mooning all over her already, on the basis of two black and white photographs.'

'The boy's at mooning age. I mooned a good deal myself, you might recall? But *mooning* is not the inevitable precursor to *matrimony*. There was correspondence too?'

'Indeed. I quite shudder to think what might be in it.'

'It's probably in *Lunese*.'

'Darius, you may persist if you will in this sort of frivolous attitude, but I don't approve at all, and it won't prevent me from taking an altogether firmer line with the children from now on. I'm going next week to fetch Irene Natasha back home without any further nonsense. I am also intending to recruit a Tutor in Political Philosophy to come here for a while. That is the sort of instruction that Julius needs. And there is no reason why a little disciplinary rain shouldn't fall into the girls' lives either. They have done enough *literature* and *music* to last a lifetime.'

'Hephzibah, I have not, perhaps, been in the habit of speaking over the years to you with anything approaching bluntness, but I am obliged to say that on this entire matter I find myself quite directly opposed to your views. Your chances of achieving success by bullying the children are negligible. With Irena Natasha it is completely doomed to failure. Try if you wish. I'll do my best not to say "told you so" when you get back. But I intend to talk to Julius in the morning, and I shall give his plans to go and study in Paris as soon as it is convenient my royal blessing.'

'I am very angry with you.'

'Yes, but you often are, my dear, and it usually upsets me, but in this matter I am utterly resolute. I am determined that the children should not be straight-jacketed, and I am convinced that you are mistaken.'

The Queen left the room in silence, and went into the bathroom. She closed the door with a good deal of firmness. In private, however, she gave vent to her feelings by snapping the head off the King's special soap, which was shaped like the Loch Ness Monster and had been a Christmas present from Irena, dissolving it in hot water in her tooth-mug and pouring the mixture over a hated cactus on the window-sill.

She gave vent to her feelings

↭ 21 ↭

Days after this regrettable scene, way across the whitened mountains and far, far distant beyond the chill flat plains beyond, a certain Bartholomew, painter, was pacing up and down on the worn patch of carpet in his London flat. Bartholomew always found that his brain worked best when he was marching to and fro like a lion in the zoo, and he now found himself in a situation that certainly demanded contemplation.

Here he was, a young man of twenty-four, alone in London, without a job or anything remotely like prospects. He knew that before long he was going to find himself speaking out loud to Irena about certain personal feelings and that there would be no drawing back from that position afterwards.

Although he cared little himself that he was penniless, he saw that the fact might well trouble a possible Father-in-law. He tried to imagine asking Irena's Father for her hand in marriage. He looked like the kind of man who would have a list of questions about her future security, bankers and settlements ready to hand. Bartholomew's position was all the more peculiar in that he knew so little of Irena's family or background.

What, in fact, *did* he know?

Her face, with complete exactness. Her hair, her voice, her size, her hands. Her character, her laughter. Of the girl herself, everything. Hard fact, however, little enough. A bit younger than himself. Oldest of five children. Fond of junk-shops and music and wandering about. Well brought up? He laughed. Certainly that. It was completely obvious that her earlier life - whatever it was - could not have been anything like his own, or much like her present life in London. Yet the same was true of him. He too had tried to escape from money and isolation into solitude in London. But even that ambition seemed to have changed too.

Perhaps he should just leave everything alone. *I am happy*, he told himself. *Why fret?*

But Irena had declared at the concert hall when he first met her that she was already happy, a little remark that had given him a lot to worry about. According to his view of the situation it should be impossible for Irena, alone, to be *happy*. And it didn't seem possible that she could already have fallen in love with anyone *else*. Somehow he knew that she just couldn't have. But she was no girl to be fluffed up and put on a mantelpiece for adoration. She was a companion, and she said most directly just what was in her head. The more he tried to look at her from an outside angle, the more clearly he understood what had happened to him.

He looked at himself in the mirror, trying to imagine how *she* might see *him*. A bony, even gaunt face with a slightly crooked nose and over-long hair. Tall and thin. Not at all frightening to children. They often thought he might be a clown in disguise.

Perhaps he was.

But perhaps her life was complete as it was, and a personal, impoverished (but highly talented) portrait painter was not what she needed at all?

It is impossible to imagine any reason at all why she should love me, he thought. Let's hope that she never comes to the same conclusion herself.

The Princess Irena Natasha was in something of a pensive mood, too. Her Father's latest letter disturbed her considerably. For some months she had deliberately refused to let herself think much about her old life at home or her possible future. Her complete concentration on her existence in London now seemed like plain selfishness, but she could not bring herself to relinquish the freedom that she had gained for herself. The further she was removed from her old life in the Palace, the more clearly she saw it for a round of endless drudgery. What was she to do?

Her living allowance, for which she had had to argue fiercely before departing, had proved quite sufficient for a Princess of modest requirements in London. Normally, of course, there was no need for her to have really anxious moments about such things. At home she had all the expected quantities of gold necklaces, pearl bracelets and jewel-studded crowns that she deserved, packed up in iron-bound chests and awaiting her return. Irena Natasha had meanwhile discovered a different pleasure in wearing jewellery that only cost her pennies, 'costume jewellery' as it was called by market-stall owners, or 'paste,' a term which she was unable to disassociate in her mind from fishy sandwiches. (The first time she heard the word, turning over a pile of Victorian brooches, it was all she could do to avoid taking a sniff.)

Now her peaceful vacuum seemed to have been shattered by several forces acting at the same moment, and she no longer felt quite so able to swim through her existence without consideration of the future.

Consideration of the future

Her Father's letter discomfited her, since its liberal acceptance of her independence made greater claims on her than the sort of strident bullying she expected from her mother. Somehow the Princess felt less ready now to ignore the demands of her royal birth.

Then, and immediately involved with such concerns, there was the question of Bartholomew. The Princess Irena Natasha felt just a twinge of worry that she had not so far said one clear word to him concerning her true identity, or its implications. That he had asked no real information of her showed tact on his part, a quality that was not lost on her. She finished her coffee, thoughtfully. Perhaps, she decided, the time has come for some open conversation…

∽ 22 ∽

Bartholomew had proposed a few days after the letters came that they might go together the next morning to visit the Monument.

'*Which* monument?' the Princess had asked, quite reasonably.

'*The* Monument,' Bartholomew had replied. 'It's a pillar with a golden ball on top, up which you can climb. It's where the Great Fire started.'

'I see. A desirable challenge in itself, you think?'

'Not to be missed. The view is worth the mountaineering.'

They met, as arranged, and went down into the Underground. Bartholomew was quiet. The Princess, too, was far from talkative.

... and went down into the Underground.

'I liked your drawing,' she said as they stood together on the escalator. 'I was proud to be able to sit for you, even though I was not even in the room at the time. My problem now is what to do with it? I mean, were I, for example, to move? I couldn't possibly just *leave* it there. And I don't see how I could quite take it with me. Walls are a sort of fixture, even in tumbledown English flats, I dare say.'

'Are you thinking of moving, then?' asked Bartholomew.

'Not instantly, but the possibility looms.'

They arrived.

'We're here,' said Bartholomew.'

'You are a wonderful guide,' said the Princess.

They began on the staircase. Round and round went the grey walls, the steps arching continuously upwards. There wasn't quite room enough for them side by side so the Princess went first, Bartholomew second, sometimes looking without meaning to at her ankles climbing above him. They were particularly slender. He felt very depressed.

∽ 23 ∽

A Council Meeting of the King's Elders was in session. King Darius always acted as chairman, as had his Father and Grandfather before him. Almost all the members were appropriately old and venerable-looking, and in comparison with the white-haired and often white-bearded nobles around the table Darius himself looked - and indeed felt - comparatively youthful.

Unless there were a national emergency Council Meetings took place once a month, customarily on the first Thursday. The rule was that anybody present could speak at any time, but the extent to which they could do so *without interruption* was entirely dependent on the King's mood.

This morning there was only a modest attendance, since the arrival of Spring had encouraged even decrepit Councillors to play truant. Nevertheless, looking round the familiar chamber, the King decided to introduce the subject of the absent Princess again there and then. Now that the Queen had announced her intention of going to retrieve her wayward daughter personally, Darius felt that the situation possessed implications beyond the bounds of the Royal Family alone. He had no doubt in his mind that Hephzibah would be unsuccessful. Before discussing anything else, then, it was imperative that the sprightliest brains in the country should come up with a concrete reason to prevent the Queen's departure and give the Princess some breathing space. He coughed for silence, and rose majestically to his feet.

'My Lords and fellow Councillors…' he began.

'Your Majesty,' came a respectful voice from the back, 'Before we get warmed up, could we have a window open, do you think? It's a really beautiful day outside.'

The King took the proposal in his stride.

'My Lords, could we, before proceeding, have a quick show of hands on this fresh air matter…?'

'Ahem, my Liege, before coming to an actual vote, might I point out that by opening the window we might expose ourselves to the very substantial danger of being overheard by *someone loitering below on the parapet?*'

'Could someone nearby please look over the parapet and see if one of these nefarious loiterers is, in fact, there?'

'Certainly, Your Majesty, if I could just take off my sword first...?'

'With respect, Sire,' intruded a more assertive voice, 'that expedient will hardly suffice for National Security. A would-be spy could wait until we had taken that precaution, watching our every move from afar through field glasses, and *then creep back underneath* and resume the sinister task with a *long flexible tube.*'

'Technically I admit the possibility, but where would anyone get a long flexible tube like that in this country? And are we really surrounded by such sinister forces?'

'... a long flexible tube like that in this country?'

'Sire, *they are everywhere.* As your Advisor on National Security I couldn't square my conscience with permitting the opening of a window during a Council Meeting and all its concomitant dangers.'

'We are deeply sensible of your prudence in this matter, Minister, but is it not possible that the deafening birdsong that I can hear even now from the Gardens might not safely mask our voices?'

'*If* it is *real* birdsong, possibly. But there are such things as *tape-recorders* on the market…'

The King paused.

'Excuse me, Your Majesty, but is all this window stuff to be entered in the minutes?'

'Just the highlights, I think, for posterity.'

Unless he acted incisively, this was not going to be a productive meeting.

'Leave it shut for now. We'll talk and think fast, and all go for a long walk afterwards. We'll enjoy our lunches more.'

The minute-taker sighed and reached for his rubber.

The King stood up again and leaned forward confidingly. He spoke in a quiet, urgent voice, and his Elders responded like seasoned hunting-dogs to his tone.

'Gentlemen, since we can consider ourselves secure, I must seek your counsel with regard to a deeply sensitive matter of state. Her Majesty, our dear Queen and my beloved wife, has announced her intention of travelling to London to round up the Princess Irena Natasha *without more ado…*

… so you see, it is imperative that we intervene…
    with *even less ado.*'

There was a thoughtful pause.

'My Liege, might one not envisage that a letter received from her Royally Absent Highness indicating that she was just leaving London that day for a long travelling holiday might suggest to the Queen that now would not be a good moment to arrive in London?'

'Indeed, a fine idea, but postage is unpredictable, and we could never get a message there and back in time to do the trick.'

'It is impossible to read such an interpretation into any part of her recent correspondence, one assumes?'

'Not with a level of authority that would seem convincing if I were suddenly to mention it now.'

'Does her Royal Highness have a telephone over there?'

'I fear not. I have written to her with that express question, but so far no answer. She is living in modest circumstances, remember, and it does seem that functional telephones are limited to particularly privileged individuals in that country.'

'In that case, Your Majesty, we must devise something *this end* that will provide a pressing reason for her to delay the trip?'

'Precisely.'

'I have an idea. Why do we not announce that the Queen's portrait is to be painted, for central positioning within the Dynastic Gallery on the Main Staircase? It can be claimed that Her Majesty is happily in her prime, and that this is an ideal moment. It might take a long time to choose an artist who will appeal to her personally, and of whose work she might approve, and then the portrait itself might require a goodly number of sittings, stretching quite unpredictably into the coming months.'

'Count Stani, this plot is *unsurpassable* in its blend of simplicity and effectiveness. I congratulate you. I cannot discern a single drawback in it. Let us consider further... We will need to imply, in the first place, that we have been planning this surprise for the Queen for a long time while we hunted for an artist of sufficient quality. We will need to produce, say, a dozen plausible candidates with outstanding portfolios more or less within twenty-four hours, so we can enlist her own help in the selection process. One or two should be obviously foreign, I would think. Can anyone help with that?'

There was a buzz of enthusiastic suggestion round the great table. Someone remembered a talented grand-nephew out in the countryside who, apparently, could draw anything, even animals. One of the Councillors had a steward who had a son who was an art student who looked, said his master judicially, artistic even from a distance. Then there was always the university. They would speak to the Dean of Arts, who must know a few painters and things.

The King called for volunteers to establish a Portrait Committee under the leadership of Count Stanislaus. They agreed to convene at the same time the following morning to report on progress. At the same time, anyone who had a bright idea to do with the plan was to make it known immediately. Darius himself undertook to mention something about a "little surprise" to the Queen during the course of that very day, before she got as far as purchasing a ticket.

Feeling a lot more light-hearted the King brought the session to a close, instructing the minute-keeper to record nothing to do with the planned operation. He had no apprehensions himself about long-range binoculars, but he knew from experience that Council Minutes had, on occasion, been surreptitiously read through by individuals other than the King's Elders, or indeed their Lord and Sovereign.

↶ 24 ↷

'Not much further, I hope,' said the Princess over her shoulder. 'So far the view is rather plain and monotonous and I am beginning to feel dizzy.'

'Should we stop for elevenses?' asked Bartholomew, solicitously.

'The manuals suggest that we should keep going. If you stop when you feel sleepy you know nothing until wet-nosed St Bernards dig you out, days later.'

'It is fortunate that your training has been so thorough, as I completely forgot to pack oxygen bottles.'

'Slack of you, but I probably have one or two in my bag.'

They continued upwards.

'I think I see light ahead,' ventured Bartholomew.

'Probably a fall of snow. We may have to bivouac.'

They reached the top of the tower and stepped out on to the balcony. It was framed all around by a freshly-painted railing. Above their heads the great golden ball that crowned the structure gleamed handsomely in the morning sunshine.

'Welcome, Madame, to our cloud-kissed abode,' said Bartholomew, scraping and bowing in an excited, squeaky voice. 'We are always ravished to welcome new visitors. Would Madame care for a guided tour? We do two-minute, twenty-minute and three-hour versions in most modern European tongues, with or without demonstrations. Memorabilia, postcards and knitted neckties are also available at our pinnacle boutique over there, and pigeon food, too, if you fancy sponsoring our high flyers.'

He bowed three times, and paused for an answer.

'I was expecting something a little more elevated architecturally. The proportions here are a trifle stumpy for my taste. Do you not have a ladder or anything to give visitors that extra boost?'

'Most of our guests seem to feel that we provide things at the right level. This is not high life as experienced in America, may I remind you.'

'True. I am justly rebuked. Perhaps on reflection this could be a satisfactory height for a tower after all.'

They reached the top of the tower

'Step this way, dear lady, and sample our *admirable* views.'

They stood, side by side, undisturbed by other visitors, far above the city that fretted and buzzed inaudibly below, and gazed out together towards the gauzy horizon.

'Irenka Natashka,' said Bartholomew suddenly, 'I love you.'

25

Julius had received a polite note from his Father requesting that he wait upon him in a small side chamber at half-past two that afternoon. To meet this appointment himself Darius would have to rush through lunch, as there had been much talk after the meeting. He was down in the Great Kitchen now, tackling a light soufflé, with his eye on pie and custard, too, thinking over his earlier conversation with the Queen. He was still certain that he was right.

There was a knock at the chamber door.
'Come in, Julius, and sit down.'
Julius duly did so. He grinned at his Father.
'What's up, Dad?'
'Julius, I have been talking to your mother, and we have had an adult exchange of views.'
'I thought you looked tired.'
'If I do, you're to blame.'
'Indeed?'
'Yes. I am awarding you your freedom and a State Allowance, to go to Paris for one year to study in your laboratory.'
'*What*?'
'Freedom, allowance, Paris, creepy-crawlies.'
'You are *serious*?'
'Entirely.'
'But I have been on the point of running away, making plans, packing maps and chocolate.'
'Well there is no need for skulduggery. You can do it publicly and comfortably, with more than chocolate in your hand luggage. I suggest you write at once to your Professor and get things moving. My only stipulations are that you remember at all times your position in life and the August Line from which you are descended, and that you communicate with us once a week. Otherwise your poor mother's imagination will run riot, and life for the rest of us here will suffer accordingly. As it is she thinks you are already engaged to a somebody in a white coat.'

...there is no need for skulduggery.

'Father, I-'

'I am teasing you. Relax. But do you think that one year will be sufficient for your studies, Julius? Would it not be more useful to read for a proper degree?'

'Possibly, but I have read a good deal already. I need experience and teaching, and the Professor's example will equip me for the work I want to do at home. I see my path clear.'

'Good, good, my boy. I cannot tell you how much I am in favour of this plan. And the Elders are right behind me, I might add. Paris is, of course, internationally famed as an entomological capital, as you need hardly tell me. Many royal houses send their offspring there to insectivoral finishing school... And perhaps sometimes you could also go to the *theatre* while you're there. You'll have the funds. And sample other things, like music, restaurants, dancing? With *bipeds*, as your mother would probably put it?'

87

'Father, I have, as befits a would-be entomologist, an open mind.'

'Excellent. Don't forget, one letter a week.'

'Do you think my including microscopic photographs with details of the daily work would help too?'

'Just what I had in mind. Plenty of hairy legs and bulging eyes. Not omitting full Latin terminology and the numbers of eggs they can produce over a weekend.'

'Leave it to me.'

'Then there is the question of your identity. I presume that you will undertake this project *incognito*? You might need some new clothes. I think, Julius, that I am going to ask the Tailor to have a word with you.'

'*Incognito* seems to be the most sensible idea, doesn't it?'

'Certainly. But there are plain clothes and plain clothes. Let's see if we can't improve things slightly. Parisian scientists probably wear designer whites about the lab.'

'I'll look into it. I'll go and write now.'

'Make your arrangements. Keep me informed.'

Julius paused in the doorway.

'Dad?'

'Yes?'

'*Thank you…*'

26

'Bartholomew,' said the Princess, after a long silence, 'there is something I have to tell you.'

'At a time like this?' said Bartholomew. 'I was just about to *propose*. I was thinking of sinking on to a single knee. You're *not* …?'

'No, of *course* I'm not. Don't be daft. It's just that I'm …'

'You *are*…?'

'… not quite like other girls.'

'This I know. You think I'd fall in love with any girl I happened to sit almost next to at a concert?'

'You misunderstand me. I am not without complications.'

'But I adore your complications. I *love* you, Irenka. I have from the minute I saw you. I am trying to manoeuvre a stretch of uninterrupted prose so that I can propose marriage to you.'

'Bartholomew-'

'Yes?'

'This cannot be possible.'

'*Absurd*. You were *made* for me. The whole thing has been planned for *centuries*. The plan culminates in your being here now, with me, alone on top of the world. It's fate. You may as well give in gracefully. I have a thousand fluent and unanswerable arguments to make mincemeat out of any statement like your last one. Why not fall gracefully into my arms like a Princess at the top of a tower being rescued by a Prince in one of those fatuous stories that parents inflict on innocent children trapped in bed?'

'But that is the trouble. I *am* a Princess. That is just the *trouble*.'

'Well, that's perfect, then. You must know how to do it.'

'No, seriously, Bartholomew, my dear would-be Prince. I *am* a Princess. I have blue blood. My name appears in those awful books as a royal 'd.' under my Father's entry. I am second in line to a *throne*. That stoutish personage whom you tugged out from under a concert seat with me is King Darius the Fourth. I am his oldest daughter. My brother Julius one day will be Julius the Fifth. They are all sitting at home having expectations of me.'

'*Pfui*. Nothing remotely like the expectations that *I* have of you. The whole affair just goes to show how right I was. I have loved you from the first exactly as if you *were* a Princess, and now in fact you tell me you are. I am not surprised in the least. It just goes to show how perceptive I am with regard to you. You make me feel like a King. Won't that do?'

'For me, but not for them, I fear …'

'Excuse me, but did you say "for me" or did I imagine it?'

'Well, look, Bartholomew…'

'Does that carefree phrase slightly imply that you might not be wholly indifferent to me at all possibly?'

'Bartholomew, you need not ask, to know that I care for you.'

'Fine. Consider it settled. How many children shall we have?'

'Bar-'

'Tell me something, Irenka. Has anyone ever asked you to marry him before this elegant attempt of my own?'

'I believe that altogether thirty-seven men have asked me to marry them at one time or another, starting when I was about nine, and continuing until two days before I left to come to England. Although for precision I should need to check my diaries.'

'And were you ever tempted by one of these despicable hounds?'

'No, Bartholomew. Not one.'

'And what about this thirty-eighth try?'

'One day I may have to-'

'Forget outside considerations. I speak to you as one person to another. Irenka, I love you. I can last no longer without telling you. Nothing else is important.' Bartholomew sank on to a knee.

Behind him there was a sudden rush of noisy excitement and a large party of tourists flooded out of the stair well into the open space behind him. Bartholomew paused, and decided to retie his shoelace. Instead of undoing it he managed to pull it into the most awkward knot he had ever seen. He caught the Princess's eye. They burst out laughing as strange bodies swarmed about them, the adults excited at the view, the children fighting for a go on the telescope fastened to the railings.

He took her hand gently and they escaped, close together, down the twisting, winding staircase to the world beneath.

the twisting, winding staircase

27

Closeted inside the Palace, the Portrait Committee was in something of a panic. The Dean of Arts had been summoned by special messenger to appear instantly at the Palace on a matter of National Importance. This was something out of the ordinary for the elderly scholar, who knew a great deal about pictures in a quiet sort of way, and liked telling other people about them, but had never argued that they might be crucial for his country's well-being. He was debating with himself whether to dig out his full academic gown, since he had been mooching about the house in old trousers and a baggy jersey of his wife's, but he had been given no time to change. The messenger had virtually kidnapped him.

He waddled slowly now down the path, his companion still urging speed, the wheezy Dean taking no notice. He was trying to envisage a national emergency that could in any way be affected by his professional knowledge.

'Come through here, Sir,' said the messenger as they turned down a side path. 'The Committee are all waiting for you.'

'Ah, Dean,' cried Count Stanislaus aloud from an upper window. 'Capital. Splendid that you are here.'

The Dean jumped. He swept a hand over what remained of his hair, and blew his nose on an antisocial handkerchief. He followed obediently up the staircase.

Despite the brightness of the day outside the drapes were pulled shut, and lamps were lit. Five eminent-looking individuals quite unknown to the Dean were seated round a circular table. There was a single empty chair, and the messenger pulled it back for him invitingly, and departed. Tea was being served from a samovar at a side table, and there was a plate of biscuits in the middle of the table. There was a note pad and a new pencil in front of each person. The Dean felt a powerful urge to take a biscuit, but fidgeted with his pencil instead.

'Dean. Welcome. Admirable that you could make it. May I introduce everybody…?'

Everyone shook hands as the Count murmured names.

'Thank you, Count. I am intrigued to find myself here slap-bang in the middle of what is clearly a plot. I regret I did not bring my cloak, although I confess to possessing no dagger, myself.'

'The plot concerns a matter of National Importance,' said the Count.

'So I understand,' said the Dean. 'Could I have a biscuit with my tea?'

'Dean, forgive me. Try the ones in the middle. They're delicious.'

'So are the others,' remarked a heavily bewhiskered man across the table. He was the Palace Archivist. 'Don't be swayed in your choice. Try one of each.'

'I think I will,' said the Dean.

'Now, Dean,' continued the Count, 'the matter is this: we need a top portrait painter, and we need one fast.'

'Well,' said the Dean, 'I'm really flattered. I used to be quite good about thirty years ago - nothing outstanding, mind you, but perfectly competent - but I'm not really sure how good I'd be now, you know. A bit rusty. I do more watercolours these days, bowls of fruit, winter landscapes, you know the sort of thing -'

'Ah, Dean, I-, we-, well, if you do feel that way we're very sorry, of course, but we understand. I wonder, could you then perhaps give us some *advice*? Allow me to explain.'

He hunched forward over the table, speaking incisively, moving his hands as he spoke.

'His Majesty has decided on a surprise gift for Her Majesty, namely a portrait in oils, to take its place among the ancestral selections in the Palace here. We need, therefore, a highly-skilled, diplomatic and fast-moving portrait painter, who can do justice to his Subject in every way, and we need one *now*.'

'But surely there are many fine portraits of the King already, more or less covering all the separate ages a man can go through. I must have seen dozens myself over the years.'

'Ah, Dean, no. It's *Her* Majesty's portrait of which I am speaking. There hasn't been a really good one, suitable to be shown to the public, say, since, I would imagine, the birth of Prince Julius, or Princess Irena. Or has there, Archivist?'

'Nothing of distinction. The idea is slightly out of fashion, I suppose.'

'Possibly. But you see the point. The Queen is, at present, in her – er *prime*, we said, didn't we, Archivist?'

'Precisely. We need a traditional and talented painter who can make that point well.'

'Quite so.'

'Furthermore, we need this artist to present himself, looking artistic to the gills, with a port- what was it, Archivist?'

'Portfolio?'

'Indeed. A portfolio. We wouldn't look at any artist who hadn't got a portfolio of his own for one minute. Well, anyway, we need this artistic-looking fellow at once.'

'But, Count, you are talking here of Art. Art cannot be hurried. And what is the rush, anyway, may I ask?'

'Dean, that is a matter of Internal Security, and I fear I cannot disclose the details even to a colleague of your standing. Heads, mine especially, would roll. Could we just leave it that – on the Highest Possible Authority – anyone who produces an artist of this kind within twenty-four hours is destined for emoluments of a highly-gratifying nature.'

'I see,' said the Dean, thinking hard. 'Let me think hard.'

'Please do,' said the Count encouragingly.

The Archivist took up the narrative.

'So far we have three candidates on our list. Two are due to present themselves here, one in a quarter of an hour, another in three quarters of an hour. The third has to come from a long distance, and won't arrive until some time this evening.'

'Excellent. But the more possibilities we can dig up, the better. If these chaps all turn out to be hopeless we will be back to square one by nightfall.'

'Back to the drawing board, don't you mean?' remarked the Dean.

They fell silent. The Dean wondered whether he could possibly undertake the commission himself. He had studied assiduously for many years, and it was true that as a young painter his portraits had commended approval at the Academy. He tried to imagine painting the Queen and having to show her the results afterwards, and abandoned the idea entirely. The trouble was he knew of no one in the country who was up to the task. It would require superhuman qualities. He found that he was rather looking forward to examining the hapless candidates.

The messenger tapped quietly three times and put his head round the door. The first candidate had arrived at the main gate. The sergeant-at-arms was bringing him over.

The Count leapt to his feet and began rearranging the chairs so that the newcomer would find himself facing a panel of judges. The biscuit tray was hidden together with the teacups, and the crumbs bundled up in the tablecloth, which was removed altogether.

'If I may, Dean,' said the Count briskly, 'I propose to conduct these interviews with a view to assessing the candidate's personality and general suitability, but you are absolutely in charge of Artistic Matters, and I should be pleased if you would just ask anything you feel is appropriate.'

'I imagine that the portfolios will largely speak for themselves,' said the Dean.

'I am an artist.'

'Oh, certainly,' said the Count, nodding. He was in fact still quite unclear as to what a portfolio actually was. His only information came from international news broadcasts, from which he knew that there were countries in which government ministers prided themselves in not having one at all.

There was a more solid knock, and the messenger reappeared, leading a short plump man in a beret and dungarees holding a great cardboard file under his left arm. He stood in the doorway, beamed generously and bowed.

'Gentlemen, you wanted an *artist*, I believe? *I* am an artist.'

'Do come in and sit down,' said the Count suavely.

The little man bounced into the room and laid his own portfolio on the table. He sat down on the elegant chair. His feet didn't quite touch the floor.

'Animal, vegetable or mineral?' he asked. 'Any tea from that samovar, incidentally, or is it just for decoration? Good background touch for a picture. You don't often see such nice ones these days.'

'It is but seldom pressed into service, I fear,' said the Count. 'Family heirloom. What do you mean by "animal, vegetable" etcetera?'

'The subject you have up your sleeve. I can do them all. Living. Dead. Scenery. Drapery. Mirrors with candlelight. Racehorses, hunted lions, storms on the ocean wa-'

'Yes, I see,' said the Count.

'Reasonable fees. Usually I charge by the square inch, depending on the medium, that is watercolour, oils, pastels, charcoal, spray cans, wode, felt-tip pe-'

'Er-,' said the Count.

The Dean leaned forward. He was enjoying himself thoroughly.

'Could we ask you to show us some of your *oeuvre*?' he asked.

The little man got off his chair and opened the great folder. It was full of photographs of his paintings. It was hard to believe they could all be the work of one man. The Dean extricated a sheet at random. It showed a great sea battle, with sailors tumbling from the rigging, and waves beating up over the prow of the man-o'-war. It was very splendid, and involved a good number of square inches of oil paint, plus a magnificent frame. The small picture that emerged beneath showed a fat baby lying on its stomach looking at itself in a mirror. It had a sickly, toothless grin. The Dean shuddered. There seemed to be paintings of every conceivable category.

'Do you perchance have any portraits?' he enquired.

'But surely. Hundreds. I'm always doing them. Full length, half length, head and shoul-'

'Could we please see a selection of specimens?'

The artist rummaged, and pulled out a fat envelope. It contained many faces. The Dean looked closely at two or three.

'Thank you indeed,' he said, 'you are remarkably productive.'

'Been professional since the age of thirteen. Natural talent. In my twenties I could paint two pictures at a time, one with each hand. Can't any more. But the hands still work.'

He looked appraisingly at his own hands, which were convincingly besmirched with paint. He gave the impression of having unwillingly torn himself away from a wet canvas to which he was itching to return.

The Count realised from the Dean's tone that he had seen all he needed to. He had himself made his decision the minute the painter had appeared in the doorway, although he wasn't going to say so. He looked round at his colleagues.

'Does anyone else have a question they would like to put?'

No one took up his offer, so with a few polite remarks the Count escorted the artist to the door and rang the bell for the messenger.

'One down,' said the Dean. He laughed.

The Count took out a handkerchief and wiped his forehead eloquently.

'I rather liked that sea battle,' said the Archivist. 'I wonder how much he would want for it.'

The Dean laughed again.

'I'd love to see him painting Her Majesty. One has to admit that he would turn in whatever we ordered. Herself at twenty-one, eating ice-cream in a mink while escaping in a trireme from a boatload of pirates...'

Count Stanislaus was more than a little outraged by the Dean's style of reference to the Queen, but he said nothing, thinking that allowance probably had to be made for artistic types.

'Gentlemen, I propose a turn outdoors to clear our heads. We have fifteen free minutes.'

They followed the Count outside. The day was still bright, but there was a fresh wind.

'What shall we do if they're *all* like that?' asked the Master-at-Arms, who had never previously been in the same room as a real live painter.

'Good question,' said the Count. 'Think again, I suppose.'

'The King is really serious about this idea. Can't we get one from *abroad*, maybe? Where do these artist people usually come from, do you know?'

They strolled about inspecting the flower-beds, and chatting among themselves. The Dean was thinking hard all over again about undertaking the portrait commission himself. It would be a fine climax to his career, and they were beginning to mention retirement in his hearing. The money would be more than useful, too. The Master-at-Arms tapped out his pipe against an outhouse wall and they all filed back into the interview chamber. The Count looked tense.

'Here we go again.'

The second artist was, inevitably, tall and thin and taciturn in the extreme.

'Do take a seat here. Have you brought some work to show us?'
'Yes,'
'Could we see some of it?'
'Yes.'
'Now, perhaps?'

The second artist reached inside his jacket and pulled out a long thin tube that must have been hidden down one leg of his trousers. In total silence he undertook the extraction of some tightly-rolled sheets, to lay them on the table. They had been encased so long that they wouldn't stay flat. In the end the Dean took one end to help him out, and opened the first reluctant scroll to the light for the others to see. It depicted an unusually-shaped woman with a pointed triangular blue nose and three eyes sitting uncomfortably in a poky three-legged chair. Colour was unevenly distributed across the picture in a way that had no obvious connection to the drawing beneath. It was labelled *Diana after the Hunt*. The Dean turned without remark to the second picture. It was clearly of the same hand, and even less comfortable to look at.

'Portraiture is your speciality, I gather?' he asked.

'Yes. But interpretive. Psychologically.'

'Yes, well, thank you indeed,' said the Count. 'Can we help you roll up your erve?'

'It's OK,' said the second artist. He rolled them deftly into a single unit and had the whole secreted about his person again with startling alacrity.

'Shall I go now?'

'Yes, well, thank you very much indeed for coming,' said the Count.

The second artist departed.

While they were still sitting in silence supplies of sandwiches and chilled white wine were brought in. Several of the Committee would be unable to be on hand later to see the third candidate, especially as no one knew quite when he would arrive. It was agreed that the Count and the Dean could be entrusted to make a first assessment themselves.

At that point, the King himself came in. He wandered over to the side table and picked up the last sandwich. The Dean stepped over to him.

'My Liege, I understand that the need for a portraitist has become an urgent matter. I just thought that I would mention that if our present endeavour proves unsuccessful, since so much is at stake from a national point of view, I should be proud to offer my own humble services. I am only a modest student of the Arts, but I know my duty and I am always at Your disposal should You ever need me.'

'Dean, we are sensible of our obligations towards you for your timely kindness and will not forget same,' said Darius, his mind altogether elsewhere.

'Your Majesty, progress is glum,' said the Count, waiting his moment, 'You need a progress report…'

It was very late by the time that the third candidate presented himself. Count Stanislas was smoking and thinking at the head of the staircase when the message came, and the Dean was, frankly, asleep in his chair.

The last artist came in very slowly. He looked about fifty, and was unpleasantly fat about the face. He had come in a hurry across half the country and now sat stolidly in his chair, his arms on the table. The Count opened the proffered folder and looked at the first picture. He spluttered slightly and turned very red. He shut the folder quickly and passed it to the Dean. The Dean took a look himself. He turned less red than the Count because he was more widely experienced in contemporary movements, but he too exhibited symptoms of embarrassment.

'Well, thank you for your trouble,' said the Count. 'The staff will see that everything is arranged for your return. Good night to you.'

The third of the Queen's would-be portraitists left without a word. The Count looked at the Dean.

'Dean, I think it's a good thing the others left.'

'Count, I agree. We are, I think, unanimous?'

The two men grinned at one another, and the Count put out the lamps.

↬ 28 ↫

The Princess was lying on the floor in her flat half-listening to music, but also deep in thought. It was early evening. Bartholomew had completely taken over the kitchen and was reading odd pages out of three cookbooks and working on something at the same time. He had found two candles for her, provided a glass of wine and left her to herself. Irena was grateful.

Irena was grateful.

She was thinking again over her earlier telephone conversation with her Father. The Princess was worried, and even had a half-formed plan to tell him about what had been happening to her. There was a particular telephone in the Palace with a number that could or would only be answered by the King himself. There

101

were many digits to be dialled, and it was strange beyond words to hear the remote ringing in her Father's study. To her delight he answered almost immediately. The Princess spoke quietly into the receiver, but hardly managed to get a word in: it had been impossible to bring up anything that was on her mind.

'Father, it is I, Irena.'

'*Irenka*, my dearest daughter, how *wonderful*. Give me the number and I'll call you back *at once*. (That was awkward as she was in the Post Office and there was a queue.) Irenka, I *cannot* just pop over there every five minutes. I have a *country* to run here… Your mother is threatening to descend on you at any minute… Look, important question: do you happen to know of any good *painters* over there? *Portrait* painters, I mean. My plan is to get your Mother to sit for a picture, so we can all have a few months off the hook. You and I *and* Julius. We've got a mad search on here, but all the candidates so far are absolute non-starters.'

'Father, since you specifically mention a *portrait* painter it is possible that I may be able to help. I'll investigate and call you tomorrow evening at the same time. All right? Speak soon…'

Bartholomew came in from the kitchen at that point carrying two plates.

'It's probably advisable to keep the lights dimmed when you're eating this,' he said. 'It's not what it is meant to be.'

There was a pause.

'It's *delicious*,' said the Princess.

'But unrepeatable,' said Bartholomew.

'I telephoned home before you came over.'

'All well at Headquarters?'

'All but one thing. There is a state of National Emergency, my Father tells me. The Red Cross are on red alert. United Nations troops are poised.'

'Really. Are you going to have to return and enlist?'

'My help has been recruited from here.'

'Will you have a secret radio and code book?'

'I am not at liberty to say. However, since you are above bribery by alien factions I think I could reveal something of our difficulty.'

'Please do.'

'We need a painter from overseas to produce the Queen's portrait.'

'You do?'

'We do. Urgently. Otherwise, she will leave the country, come straight here, and try to force me to return with her.'

'This is undeniably an emergency. Let me think hard.'

He poured more wine, and lay back looking at the ceiling.

'Irenka, do you have a photograph of your Mother with you?'

'I do. Let me try to find it.'

'I mean, does she exhibit the range of characteristics conventional in a human model?'

'Hard to answer. She is regarded as striking in appearance. She is a woman of undoubted character. Julius calls her the "power before the throne." I think she would have preferred to be Queen Victoria.'

'Sounds endearing.'

'The very word.'

Irena pulled out an envelope of small photographs and found two of her mother. She handed them over. Bartholomew sat up and took them, gingerly.

'She won't bite,' said the Princess.

'We'll see,' said Bartholomew.

He studied the photographs in silence with great care under the table lamp.

'I shouldn't have known her for your Mother,' he remarked.

'I look like my grandmother on the other side, apparently. I imagine what they want for the Palace is a full-blown oil portrait in traditional style by a famous foreign artist to record her nearly as she is. Probably the larger the better. With a truly splendid gold frame.'

'I have never painted a portrait twenty feet high, but I could try. I'll have to save up for the paints. I am not famous, admittedly, but I am terrifically *foreign* and I can get a likeness.'

'I know. Even on a wall. *Could* you do it, Bartholomew?'

'For you I could do anything. Would you like to see my portfolio?'

'I think yes. Now we've been introduced.'

'It's in the garret where I endure hunger, unless the rats have eaten it. We could go tomorrow. You've never seen it. I was going to invite you anyway.'

29

Next morning there was a letter for the Princess half under the mat. It had no stamp. The reason was it had merely come down the stairs:

> Dear Your Majesty,
> It is ages since we bumped into you in our hall even though I have been periodically going up and down in the hope of doing so. I write to tell you that I have composed a special piece of music for you in the hope that I might be appointed Court Musician in due course. Failing that, if you would care to venture upstairs in person I could offer you the first performance. I hope that all is well with the Dynasty at large. The piece is for three orchestras at once, but there is a version for single keyboard. If you wish to hear a bar or two do let me know. I am thinking of taking a well-earned musical rest in case my genius runs out.
> Yours with every token of respect,
> Belshazzar.

The Princess smiled to herself on reading this. It was true that she hadn't seen her composer for many days.

> Dear Belshazzar [she wrote there and then],
> I shall be enchanted to attend the very first recital of my eagerly-awaited new work. I shall certainly put in a word for you in support of your application to my Father, although I should think it must be two hundred years since the post of Court Composer was last filled. There would be drawbacks that ought to be considered in advance. You will have to wear the time-honoured uniform. I imagine it would involve stiff squeaky fabric, breeches and lacy cuffs. Also, the salary might be pitched at an eighteenth-century level. Nevertheless you are not a man to be put off by such material considerations, I am sure.
> I remain, in all sincerity yours,
> The Princess Irena Natasha.

She had the day to herself before seeing Bartholomew in the early evening at his studio. What should she do with her time now, she wondered…

Bartholomew, at that same moment, was climbing the stairs to his studio. He had remembered when he woke up that he really ought to check what state it was in before the Princess arrived. It was about two weeks since he had last been there, and he realised that he had done no painting at all since the day he had met Irena. *What did that mean?*
His subsequent output consisted merely of some private doodles on an envelope or two and her quick portrait on the kitchen wall. The familiar room greeted him as he unlocked the door, the strong smells undiminished, but there was a layer of dust over everything, and it did not feel like a living workplace at all. There were some abandoned brushes that would now be useless. He sighed. What would he do if he had lost all his skill over the last fortnight?
Perhaps he wouldn't be able to paint at all, let alone manage Queen Victoria in a snow-bound castle. He picked up a notebook full of sketches and heads. They weren't so terrible, but they didn't look as competent in his eyes now as when he had just finished them. There was a half-finished still-life on the easel, in particular, that struck him as devoid of any merit whatsoever.
He tried to imagine how his studio would appear to the Princess. It was, at any rate, full of convincingly artistic materials. There was an old leather sofa spilling its stuffing, which would have been roomy enough for three people but for the quantity of props heaped on it, odd items that Bartholomew had picked up over the years to incorporate in his paintings. Several patterned rugs, now so grubby and stained that the original designs could hardly be distinguished, covered the floor.
It was chilly in the studio. It was cold there almost all year round, almost impossibly so in winter, and the lightness of the air outside at that moment hardly penetrated. He shivered, thinking that he would have to dig out his fingerless gloves if he wanted to work today.

...full of convincingly artistic materials

Maybe I should try something right now, he thought, just *to see*.
Bartholomew took the unloved still-life off the easel and turned its face to the wall. He lit the gas under the kettle, and found a small unused canvas on a stretcher. He propped it up conveniently

and hunted round for some brushes. He mixed some dark paint with turpentine and, using a favourite brush, began to sketch in a face. It was clearly a girl's face. Before long the face was entirely recognisable. Bartholomew bent close to the canvas, gripping the slender handle, gazing at his work, breathing life into it. Before long he was utterly lost to the world.

The doorbell rang far below. Twice. Bartholomew looked up. It was growing dark in the studio and there was someone downstairs. In a rush he remembered that Irena was coming to see him. He looked at his watch. She was exactly on time and he had been painting for nearly seven hours without realising it. He was starving and his back ached. There was no time now for any of the preparations that he had planned that morning. He switched on the light and ran down the stairs two at a time to snatch open the front door.

Irena Natasha was actually standing there on his doorstep. She smiled at him uncertainly. He looked altogether different from the sleepy cook of the day before, and slightly frightening. He opened the door wide, staring at her.

'Hello, Bartolomeo,' she said gently. 'Are you not expecting me?'

'You've been here all day,' said Bartholomew.

He put out his hand to touch her arm.

'Come up. See the mess. I have the world's least comfortable furniture. Are you hungry?'

They climbed the staircase in silence. Bartholomew pushed open the door and invited the Princess to precede him into the room.

The spotlight in the ceiling shone directly on to the wet canvas in the centre of the darkening room. He had finished the face and neck, but only blocked in part of the background, leaving the borders irregular and white. The face was framed by untidy hair. The Princess stood before her portrait. Her own hair that evening happened to be pulled back tight and held in place by a red elastic band. She gazed at the painting. Its sincerity and tenderness alike were unmistakable. And it was her own face. She looked at Bartholomew. He was staring at her again as if he had never seen her before.

'I'm absolutely ravenous,' he said. 'Let me take you out for a cheap but filling dinner.'

'You're on,' said the Princess. She looked quickly round the studio. 'You have persuaded me entirely.'

He turned out the lights and double-locked the door. It was dark on the stairs going down and he held her arm tightly. In fact he was slightly hurting her but she said nothing.

℘ 30 ℘

Bartholomew yawned heavily as they made their way from the restaurant to the bus stop, and was silent at her side. The Princess didn't mind as she was running over in her mind what to say to her Father to secure the contract for her artist to paint the famous portrait. It would need to be carefully done.

Over dinner she had gathered some overdue snatches of biographical information. Bartholomew, she had learned, had been regarded as a highly promising portraitist by his teachers, but after an absolutely explosive argument one day with his professor he had marched straight out of the school, never to return. While probably able to make a living painting commercial canvases for rich friends and acquaintances of his parents, he had refused to settle for that, and had spent the intervening eighteen months visiting exhibitions and galleries and painting erratically in private, showing his work to no one at all. He now existed frugally on a small sum of money left him by his grandmother. His work during this period had improved rapidly, and the conviction that he had it within himself to be a great painter was undiminished. This solitary existence meant that he had never had a real exhibition of his paintings, and no record of public reaction. Could her own recommendation suffice for the King to invite him to the Palace as a plausible candidate?

The case must be put casually but effectively. As there were no real local candidates her position would be a little stronger than it might have been, but she didn't want Bartholomew to travel all the way to her Father's castle for an unsuccessful interview. Then she remembered her own new portrait. If he could capture the Queen's character with half that skill, she thought, the result would exceed all their expectations. All she could think was that it was imperative for him to get the commission. If he were invited to the Palace for several weeks there would be no need to explain everything to her Father.

Bartholomew had fallen asleep beside her. She had to wake him to get off the bus, and he was grumpy. He led the way down one or two side streets, still yawning hugely.

'Key,' she suggested.

A key appeared, eventually, and proved to match the lock.

They were inside the house.

'Collapse on the sofa,' said the Princess,' I'll make some more coffee.'

Her host acted upon her suggestion with a speed that some might have thought unchivalrous. With a laugh the Princess went into the kitchen.

It was evident at first glance that Bartholomew's kitchen was that of a bachelor. There was a bit of washing up to do, the remnants of one or two quick-release breakfasts. Letters from many places were lying about, several still unopened, and other interesting-looking papers that the Princess refrained from investigating. She saw pencils and drawings everywhere, including several of herself. The best one was pinned over the sink, and showed her looking over her shoulder at something out of the picture. There was a small dog at her heels looking, in turn, up at her.

She was deeply struck by these private drawings. What will he think of my own pictures, she wondered then, not for the first time. She touched nothing, but was unable to resist reading a short letter in minute pencilled script that had been lying on the table, displaced by her sleeve on to the floor:

Irenka Natasha my Irenka
I love you only
Your obedient servant and admirer,
Bartholomew.

Considering that it was addressed to her she was tempted to put it in her pocket but she put it back. She found the kettle. The kitchen was full of personal things and she felt that perhaps she should not really be there without him, but she didn't believe Bartholomew would mind. There was a clarity and sincerity about everything, even the washing-up. She was curiously relaxed. By herself, in that room, it came to her that she had nothing to fear.

'… Yes I *have*. I have seen his work *myself*. It is remarkable. I don't believe that we could do better,' said the Princess.

'I have seen his work myself.'

'I am explaining to people here that you have been very fortunate in securing the services of a well-known society painter.'

'That is the case.'

'Who happens to have an unanticipated gap in his timetable at this point due to a cancellation for reasons that we will not go into.'

'Indeed.'

'I think that armed with this intelligence I can probably face your Mother.'

'You could perhaps inform her that when I went to see his work today in his London studio he produced a small oil study of me there and then. He has an outstanding flair for a likeness. He could bring this painting with him as a sample of his abilities, could he not?'

'That would certainly be a sound move, although your Mother will probably retort that she can hardly remember what you look like, so how could she judge your picture? And, in addition, perhaps a list of other public commissions that he has fulfilled lately? I have the Dean of Arts breathing down my neck.'

'I think that society painters tend to be rather unforthcoming about such things. Like doctors about their patients. Could you not simply imply that he is widely celebrated for his discretion in such matters? Besides, why should we not have a free hand to do as we wished? In my view Mother would be fortunate to sit for such a painter.'

'I quite agree. Don't worry; I can be regal when necessary. And he could come over as soon as *next week*? I'll prepare Her Majesty tonight. You estimate he will need about one month from start to finish? Perhaps you could ask him to send a letter accepting my commission, letting us know about the fee. Such expenditure will certainly be met out of State Moneys, no question at all. It will go through like clockwork in Council. This is absolutely no time for penny-pinching. Might a travel advance be appropriate, do you imagine? When I have heard from your end I'll have the paperwork produced.'

They exchanged a few further remarks.

'Oh, and what is his name?' asked the King as an afterthought.

'Monsieur Bartholomew.'

'Mmm. Certainly sounds like a real painter.'

∽ 31 ∾

Darius was extremely pleased with his eldest daughter, and was looking forward to letting it be known in certain quarters that he had negotiated this tricky diplomatic matter entirely unaided by his staff. First, though, he must break the good news to the Queen. He had hardly seen her for two days, and was unsure how advanced her plans might be. He went straight to their bedroom.

His wife was propped up against the pillows in their ancestral bed, fast asleep, with a large London guide-book open on her lap. He looked at her with fondness. She was, very slightly, snoring. It was half-past midnight. Judging by the state of the room she could not be planning to leave the following morning. He got in beside her and lifted the book gently off her knees. It was open at the National Gallery. Very appropriate, he thought sleepily. Why *don't* we start a National Gallery here? The Queen's new portrait could be the first acquisition…'

Hephzibah awoke before her husband. She felt just as irritable as on the previous day. She looked crossly down at Darius. He opened one eye and looked at her.

'*Darling*,' he said affectionately.

'Yes?' said the Queen, looking for her slippers.

'I've got some rather special news for you.'

'You're abdicating?'

'As yet no. Why, would you like to take over?'

'Someone has to run things round here.'

The conversation didn't quite seem to be proceeding as planned. He decided to try another approach.

'We had a meeting of Council in the last few days.'

'Load of old fogies. The whole system should be abolished. Totally inept, the whole lot of them. Deaf, blind -'

'Oh, then you won't want to hear about their proposed gesture with regard to Yourself?'

'Gesture? Myself?' The Queen looked up.

'Yes. We realised that quite soon it will be your birthday, and that it has been an unforgivable length of time since you had a proper *portrait* painted. There was a unanimous vote that we should do something about that as soon as possible, no expense spared.'

'Portrait?'

'Exactly. Full length. In state dress, with your favourite crown and all your jewels. In oils. In a big golden frame.'

'But-'

'You're probably going to say that there is no one in the Kingdom of a calibre capable of producing such an important work. We've thought of that. We're bringing over a much sought-after society painter from London who has carried out many such commissions. Top-notch man. Discreet. One of my agents looked into it for me. He has just sent a message asking how soon your artist should arrive, and when the first *sitting* might be convenient for you.'

'Oh, really.'

'Yes. I gather that a major work of this kind could easily take up to a month. We're lucky he had a cancellation. Some elderly subject... er... passed on. Creating an unexpected interlude in a very busy schedule.'

'*Schedule*? You make him sound like a bus company.'

'By schedule I mean he is always much in demand. Society painters have a list like a dance-card. One cannot normally just step in with an impromptu request.'

'Has he ever done a full-length Queen before?'

'At least three quarters of one European Princess, I gather. But obviously no one of your own qualities and splendour. I imagine the challenge will be most gratifying to a real artist.'

'You do. Could I be shown some of his finished work before I commit myself?'

'Naturally, my dear. Oh, and I was thinking that if the result is as fine as we expect, we might... use the Head on a new... *Postage Stamp*, too. Like... Queen Victoria.'

The Queen paused.

'All this would mean that I should have to postpone my going to London. What about Irena Natasha?'

'We'll see. I have asked her to send me a telephone number so that we can speak to her in the meanwhile.'

'I shall have to have my hair done properly, and the white ball dress, if we are to use that, will need some attention. You remember all the sequins...? It may need some adjustment.'

... may need some attention.

'*Hardly*, darling, surely.'

'There is a great deal to be done if you are going to send the message right away.'

'I should set things in motion, then?'

'Well, do. Irena Natasha will just have to wait until my picture is finished.'

'She will be disappointed, Hephzibah.'

'Undoubtedly, but this is a matter of state. Personal considerations have to take second place at such times, as she will be the first to acknowledge. You know, Leepy, I wonder, thinking about the new stamps, whether we shouldn't have several values in different colours?'

She fell silent.

'What is the artist's name, may I ask?'

'Monsieur Bartholomew.'

'Mmm. At least he sounds like a real painter.'

32

Artist Bartholomew arrived at the Palace thirty-six hours later in the highest of spirits.

He had been alarmed at the quantity of luggage he seemed to need for a month's painting, and very reluctantly left his trusted easel behind when the Princess pointed out that the Palace carpenters could make him a comfortable new one. He had all his paints, brushes and bottles in one battered suitcase, and an immense roll of canvas too.

The Princess had come to the station to see him off.

'I *love* you, remember,' said Bartholomew on the platform. 'This is my official challenge. I am going off to beard the dragon in its lair in a difficult and far-flung foreign country. If I come back alive after one month I don't see how you can possibly refuse me your hand.'

'Have you been talking to someone about my Mother, Bartholomew?'

'I was speaking figuratively. If they cut off my head, of course, I'll give in gracefully. Otherwise, once the paint's dry, I shall fly to your window and throw down my brushes at your feet.'

'Perhaps you'll win so many commissions on the strength of the portrait that you'll forget all about me and settle there permanently.'

'Impossible. You fill my every second. Just keep in mind that I love you above all other women, including all other Princesses.'

'Come back safely, Bartholomew. Good luck with them all. If you need a *confidant* there stick to Julius. Will you bring back my own portrait when you return?'

'I might. If you're good. My train arrives... One little month, my beloved Princess.'

He had kissed her hand once, touched her cheek, and clambered aboard.

In the Palace his luggage was whisked away and Bartholomew was shown to his rooms by the Chamberlain. He had all to himself a small dressing-room and (by his previous experience) the most *luxurious* bedroom. The windows were tall and narrow, as if to allow the bow and arrow of a defender. He flung himself on the bed and began a letter to the Princess immediately. He was determined to write to her every day.

There was a knock. The Chamberlain put his head round the door and asked politely if Bartholomew thought he would be comfortable.

'Ideally. When shall I meet Their Majesties, can you tell me?'

'Tomorrow morning. The King wishes to see you first, at eleven o'clock. I will take you to him myself. He will then present you to Her Majesty, so that you can have a little conversation. I shall later today introduce you to Her Majesty's Lady-in-Waiting so that you can sort out whatever may be necessary directly with her. I shall send an equerry to escort you. Oh, one thing, do you know how to bow?'

'I am sorely out of practice.'

'I shall instruct him to give you some hints. If you ever need anything in this Palace, incidentally, Monsieur Bartholomew, come and find *me* at once. Let's go down to the Kitchens now for a bite of lunch.'

'Your Majesty, may I now present the painter, Monsieur Bartholomew?' said the Chamberlain from the doorway, and Bartholomew found himself once more face-to-face with Irena's Father.

He had chosen to wear his most artistic black clothes and, not surprisingly, he looked especially tense and gaunt. Darius looked at him. He recognised him instantly, but betrayed no sign of doing so, welcoming him with a smile and an expansive gesture. For a split second the uncharitable thought crossed his mind that Irena might be playing a trick on them all, but then, on reflection, Bartholomew did *look* quite like a painter.

Bartholomew divined entirely what was in the King's mind, and without a word produced from behind his back his painting of the King's oldest daughter, holding it out like an offering. It was unpolished and unfinished, but it left Darius speechless.

'Monsieur Bartholomew,' said the King at length, 'that is an absolutely beautiful painting. I should be happy to pay you a great deal of money for it for our National Collection.'

'I fear that it is not for sale, Your Majesty,' said Bartholomew gravely. 'It belongs to the Princess herself.'

'Pity,' said the King. 'Let us hope then that you can favour us with an additional manifestation of your magic.'

'Your Majesty may rest assured that I shall do my utmost to give satisfaction.'

'If you produce something half that good you shall,' said the King quietly.

'The Princess Irena is well and happy,' said Bartholomew. 'She is thriving in London.'

'I entirely agree with you,' said the King, 'but we are a minority here who approve of the arrangement. More anon, perhaps. Do you happen to play billiards?'

'Keenly but poorly,' said Bartholomew.

'We are well matched, then. We'll try a game later. Now I should introduce you to Her Majesty. She is very much looking forward to meeting you. You have not, of course, met before?'

'That has not so far been my privilege, but I have seen two photographs.'

'Irena Natasha takes after my own mother,' said the King, inconsequentially.

He came over to Bartholomew still holding the painting, and they left the room together.

'Her Majesty is in the Ballroom. Shall we go over and find her?'

They walked down several passages, crossed a courtyard and turned into a separate part of the great building.

'It's down here,' said Darius.

They stepped into the State Ballroom. At first they didn't notice the Queen, for she was standing on the other side of the great room, her face turned three-quarters to the tall windows, staring out into the distance. She was wearing a long formal dress that the King hadn't seen before, with gloves to the elbow. They approached quite close before she turned, as if startled from a reverie, to gaze at them. Darius experienced a strong desire to laugh at his wife's theatricality, but no one would have guessed so from his smooth introduction.

'My dear, may I present Monsieur Bartholomew of London, your painter? Monsieur Bartholomew, Her Majesty Queen Hephzibah.'

Bartholomew, with great presence of mind, went down on one knee and kissed the Queen's proffered hand in its glove.

'Your Majesty, a great honour,' he said in a quiet, respectful voice.

'Monsieur Bartholomew has brought but a single piece of work to show you, but I think you will find it revealing,' said the King. He was still holding the picture in one hand, and he held it up and showed it to the Queen.

'... looking at this little picture.'

She looked long and hard at the painting without a word.

'It is not finished, I suppose?' she said eventually.

'Indeed not, Your Majesty. I dashed it off when your daughter came to my studio the other day, to ask about your official portrait. It is just a study, to get a likeness.'

He grimaced inwardly saying this, for the painting was the best piece of work he had ever created.

119

'I hope you will cover *all* the canvas when you do *my* portrait,' said the Queen.

'Absolutely, Your Majesty. An official portrait is altogether a different matter from a superficial sketch like this. I would imagine working up a couple of preliminary studies first, just to get the feel of the painting, but I guarantee that with the proper picture there will be *absolutely no white canvas* showing through.'

The King looked swiftly at Bartholomew, but his face showed nothing but sincere concern mixed with respect.

'Fine,' said the Queen. 'I must say you do seem to be able to show what somebody looks like. I can almost hear Irena Natasha's voice, looking at this little picture.'

Bartholomew felt very peculiar to hear the words "Irena Natasha" pronounced so coldly.

'Splendid,' said Darius. 'The Chamberlain will take Monsieur Bartholomew to the Lady-in-Waiting this afternoon, and they can organise the sittings at your convenience.'

'I should be very happy to begin tomorrow morning, if appropriate,' said Bartholomew. 'I need to *look* at Her Majesty, if indeed a man may look at a Queen?'

The King laughed.

'Come with me, young man, before you get yourself into trouble.'

☙ 33 ❧

'… and one other point I ought to mention,' said Bartholomew politely to the Lady-in-Waiting, 'is that there is no need for Her Majesty to wear her full regalia for the early sittings. A sweater and jeans will do. Although I should be glad if she could have her crown handy. I must capture the way she holds her head, if that is not a treasonable ambition.'

'I am certain that Her Majesty's wardrobe, fabled though it is, features no single pair of jeans. Sweaters we can manage.'

'Or we could think of a sable bikini?'

'Monsieur, I shouldn't dare. Her Majesty is not celebrated for her sense of humour.'

'Oh dear. Does that mean I have to be permanently on my best behaviour? It is quite unnatural for me to remain too formal with a model. One is looking for the real person, and must therefore be a real person. I'm usually especially pugnacious with reigning Queens.'

'Monsieur Bartholomew, I saw the painting that you did of our Princess. It's simply marvellous. I couldn't stop looking at it. You must really know her well to have painted her like that. It's almost as if you –'

'Not another word, Maria.'

'Tell me, then, Monsieur is she really *happy* over there in London? I do miss her. I have known her for a very long time, and she is my pride and joy. In all that time she has always behaved exactly like a true Princess.'

'I have observed the same characteristic myself. Yes, I do believe she is happy in London. I have often seen her laughing, if that is any clue, and she eats properly, I am pleased that you like the painting. Let us hope that you approve of the next one.'

'Well, we're all very excited about it, I can tell you. Especially Her Majesty. The whole thing has done her the world of good. She has been very tense lately.'

'Just wait till I've finished with her. Once I've been rude a few times and got paint on her dress we'll see how relaxed she is. Is she technically empowered these days to say "off with his head!" by the way?'

'You needn't worry. The Executioner has just gone for his fortnight in the Algarve. I must say that She and I are really looking forward to tomorrow…'

'Could I ask you to hold your head just … *so*? A little higher? Perfect! Perfect!'

So saying Bartholomew grinned at the Queen, who scowled in return in a most unladylike fashion.

'Now, we must decide on the *tone* we are striving for here. The five obvious options are Patroness-of-the-Arts, Worried-but-Youthful-Looking-Mother-of-Five, Empress-of-the-Icy-Wastes, Philosopher-cum-Poetess, or Hater-of-Portrait-Painters-with Venom.'

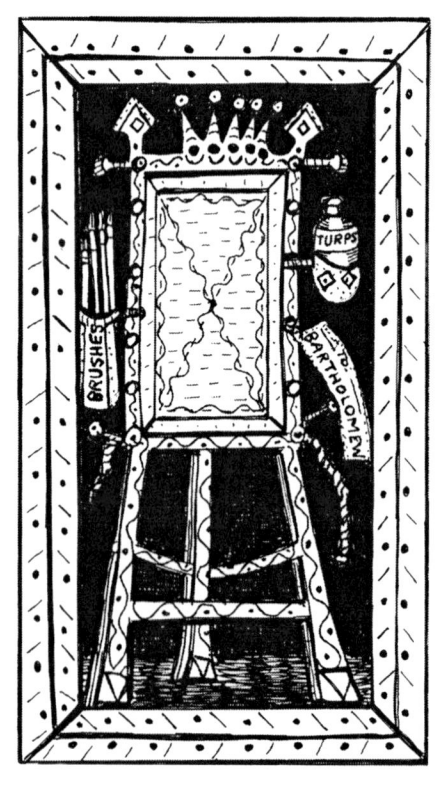

… a work of art in itself.

Despite herself the Queen smiled.

'A-ha!' said Bartholomew. 'Light in your eye. That is what I need. Light in your eye.'

He bent again over his new easel. The easel was a work of art in itself. The Court Carpenters had come up with a working sketch within minutes, and the finished product, adjustable, sturdy and inlaid with the King's motto, had appeared the following afternoon outside his door, propped against the wall like a parcel that would not go through the letterbox.

'Is it heavy, your crown?' asked Bartholomew, painting broad strokes with a nearly dry brush.

'This one, not so bad. It's a comfortable domestic model for wear about the Palace, watching rounders matches, sitting for portraits, that sort of thing. The *state* crown is awful. I have shooting stars in my left shoulder for days each time I wear it.'

'We'll have to try and spare you as much torture as possible. I should hate to become a pain in your neck. Do you play a lot of rounders, may I ask?'

'Myself? *Certainly.* Whenever I get the chance. The King, too, is forever slipping into sports clothes and tossing a medicine ball around. Take care you aren't bludgeoned into early morning exercises yourself. We are, as I hope you realise, a primarily *athletic* family. This sort of *cultural* activity – she waved vaguely at the back of Bartholomew's canvas – is a rare outbreak among us.'

Bartholomew grinned at the Queen. He felt rather pleased with himself to have goaded her into such conversation.

ॐ 34 ॐ

They worked dedicatedly every day. Bartholomew was keen to start as early as possible, but the Queen was reluctant at the idea of rising daily at six and forgoing a decent breakfast. They compromised finally on half-past nine, with plenty of breaks to prevent boredom or pins and needles.

Usually, when working from a model, Bartholomew preferred to work in silence. Now, in the preliminary sittings while he was planning the painting, he found himself oddly talkative. The Queen, on her part, found the close concentration of an intense young man on her facial structure to be unexpectedly agreeable. Bit by bit she began to treat her long daily sessions as a chance to talk about things that were troubling her. After a day or two of more general conversation the Queen got on to the subject of the Crown Prince Julius. Julius, he learned, was a big disappointment to his mother. She was furious at the way in which his Father always took his side, and she disapproved volubly of his plans to go to Paris.

Bartholomew, concentrating, was extraordinarily interested in the details of Irena's family, and soon learned to encourage the Queen. Small noises that indicated attentiveness usually sufficed to prod her into further thinking out loud.

He found himself struggling against the paint. He knew of old that fighting was useless. He put down his brush.

'Time for the medicine ball?' he asked.

The Queen leapt off her stool like a young girl and laughed.

Bartholomew was hoping that sooner or later she would bring up the subject of Irena herself, but it was several more days more before the Queen even alluded to her absent daughter. She had been complaining that nobody sympathised with her worries about marrying off her dependants.

'You can have no idea,' she remarked one morning, 'of the sense of responsibility they bring. One cannot just ignore the question of their future, especially the older two. The younger two girls, now, are wooed by suitors in this Castle just like their older sister, and neither of them will look twice at anybody. I go to a lot of trouble to invite eligible young men to come and stay, but my daughters just look at me and giggle whenever I try to talk to them like adults. And they are supposed to be Princesses. I sometimes think that they couldn't produce a serious thought between them if the Kingdom depended on it. And Irena is even worse. A highly rebellious young woman, with no sense of her obligations at all. I pity the man who eventually does marry her. She just swanned off to England without a by-your-leave, or a twinge of self-criticism, living in some hovel, pretending that she is a commoner and mixing with Lord-knows-whom. Oh, I forgot that you are acquainted with her. Well, perhaps you will think me intolerant, but in my view a Princess in her position cannot just disregard the demands on her made by the State. She should be married off by now, and married appropriately, not living alone in a strange city.'

'... just look at me and giggle ...'

Bartholomew could not have agreed more with this last observation, but did not say so. He made a listening sort of sound, and concentrated visibly on his palette.

'The thing that really annoys me,' pursued the Queen, shifting slightly on her perch with an apologetic glance at her Court Painter, 'is that Irena has had such good offers. A girl cannot afford to let such opportunities pass by.'

Bartholomew picked up a paint-rag and wiped the handle of his best long brush.

'Good offers?' he said after a pause.

'Oh, yes indeed. High born, wealthy young men, from the most ancient families. Some of them had perfectly good profiles; one had a chin, even.'

'That helps, I suppose,' said Bartholomew, bent over his colours.

'Well, you know my own mother always said that arranged dynastic marriages often turned out better that the other spontaneous kind. People learn to get on when they have no choice.'

Bartholomew was tempted to ask the Queen whether that had happened to her, but kept silent.

'May I ask whether you are yourself married, Monsieur Bartholomew?'

'I? No. I am alone,' replied Bartholomew.

'Oh,' said the Queen. 'Well, you are still young, are you not?'

'I am nearly at the marrying age,' said Bartholomew, 'but I have strong views. I should marry only for love.'

'Love! Don't speak to me about love! You sound like Irena Natasha. Princes and Princesses do not marry for love in this world, any more than do sensible people.'

'I fear that I am unable to agree with Your Majesty that love is to be so entirely dismissed from the scheme of things.'

'Well, it would be perfectly appropriate in your case. You are an *artist* and are entitled to believe in *romance*. I am merely speaking of those who must serve a higher cause than their own inclinations.'

'You think, Ma'am, that such a description could not perhaps also apply to Art?'

The Queen fell silent at this, and Bartholomew felt it was time to change the subject.

'What about the Princess Irena? Does she write to you all from London?'

'Only to her Father. They're in *cahoots*, those two. I am sure that she writes to him far more often than to the rest of us. He's nearly as bad as she is. He'd be off somewhere living in a romantic shack himself if he had half a chance.'

It was time by then for another interlude. The Queen descended a bit stiffly, and called for tea. Bartholomew winked at the serving-maid from behind his easel, and, since the Queen wasn't looking, she winked at him in return.

∞ 35 ∞

The Princess whose conduct had been so criticised by Queen Hephzibah was, at that moment, lying on her bed writing to Bartholomew. She was not quite convinced that she would ever post the letter, but she was certainly in the mood for conversation. She thought again of Bartholomew trying to propose in a passing moment of privacy, and started laughing. For two weeks she had seen him every day, and had never had the time to take stock of what her feelings might be.

Bartholomew had now been gone for nearly a week. For the first two or three days she didn't think much about anything, cooking, reading or going for unadventurous walks. She refused to look inside herself and ask any questions. This morning, however, she was in a different frame of mind. Something inside her had absorbed the idea that she had received a proposal of marriage, a proposal which was in every way unlike those that she had received before.

> *My dear and most valiant Knight* [she wrote],
> *I am consumed with curiosity to learn how you are in that distant and perhaps strange world, in the course of your heroic challenge. London is lonely without you. I calculated today just how much time we have spent in one another's company, and now I am forlorn without you here to make me laugh. I talk to you, to make up for it. Do you, I wonder, hear? I wonder if you will write to me? I wonder how you feel. I wonder how I feel.*
> *Your forlorn but unflagging Princess,*
> *I. N.*

She wrote this message in small writing on the back of a postcard of a London bus, which she then put in an envelope. She addressed it in unidentifiable handwriting and found a stamp in her purse.

He would be home in three weeks and two days, if everything went according to plan. Twenty-three days seemed, suddenly, an unreasonably long time. Mope. Droop. *Enough* of this, she thought. Time to do some drawing. And so it was: what *had* become of her own work lately...?

Mope. Droop

So, the Princess went off that afternoon to her art-supplies shop. It was risky to go *inside* too often because it was crammed on three floors with the most tempting possible items for an artist. Today, however, more than window-shopping was called for. She marched in and went straight to the back of the shop where she knew the rows of coloured inks were. The bottles had delicate painted labels with scenes of windmills or milkmaids that always enticed her, and since she was now concentrating on *drawing* she had a good excuse to buy a few more. It was childish, she knew, to hanker after the whole set, especially as she would never be able to use them all, but there was an old spice-rack in her kitchen that would hold quite a number, and she hummed to herself as she re-inspected the range of colours and shades.

Then she needed new nibs. The Princess preferred *very* thin ones to do her lines, and thicker ones to block in tree-trunks, or shady buildings under a night sky. A plan was forming at the back of her mind that she might do a whole collection of drawings on one subject, almost like illustrating a book. Then she would have something proper to show Bartholomew when he came home. She would draw every day and keep all her work in a folder. She was not the sort of Princess to sit about in the middle of London and *pine*, after all. No, she would work as hard as she could. There were some beautiful white cardboard boxes full of charcoal sticks very close by. And a tempting coloured tin of pastels. Irena had never really tried drawing with either, so they too were added to her purchases pile. Then she went upstairs for a thick pad of Artist's Paper, and thought she had better get two while she was there.

Charcoal was altogether too messy for such new white sheets of paper, and anyway it was hard for a Princess to put up for long with black, smudgy fingertips. The pastels were even worse, reminding her of her old blackboard with sums in the Palace Schoolroom. She would stick to her pretty bottles of clean inks. The Princess sat at her table and lined them up in a neat row, next to a cup of black tea and an egg-cup of nib-water.

What to illustrate? She was always drawing trees, people from a distance, the smoky surround of solid brick and rows of London houses. She had drawn everything that could be seen out of her windows, many times. What now? Something from life, or out of her head? The easiest thing would be to illustrate a *book*. That *was* an idea. To take scenes or characters from someone else's mind and bring them to life on the page... But *which* book? It seemed silly to draw pictures for a book that had already been published with someone else's pictures. What was Bartholomew's favourite book? She had no idea. Maybe it would be easier to write a story herself. The Princess wrinkled her forehead. She was supposed to be an *artist*, not an *author*. And anyway, what could she possibly write about? *Castles? Being a Princess?*

Chapter One, she wrote, and drew some entwined leaves and grapes around the capital letters.

There once lived a giraffe, she continued, promptly, who would not stop growing. It wasn't so noticeable when he was young, but before long he stood out among the giraffes of his own age, and he maintained his lead from that point on. His legs grew and his neck grew and he began to feel self-conscious and uncomfortable.

One of the new nibs was perfect for giraffe blotches. She couldn't quite visualise what a giraffe's feet should look like. But it might not be so hard to find a story. Her drawing pen seemed to have taken her over.

His mother said proudly that he stood head and shoulders above his peer group, and was destined for high places. His father, in a world of pedigree legs and necks, was much taken aback at his son's development. He had always been just a tad undersize for an adult male giraffe - although considerably over the head of Gan-glee's mother, of course. Gan-glee was able to reach the highest leaves unchallenged, and nobody could touch him in races. Such things were some compensation, but after a long day his neck ached and -

The Princess decided to work out the whole story first, and then plan the pages, doing all the pictures and inking the words in between afterwards. This was a good decision. It was something to mention in her diary, which she had also been neglecting dreadfully recently. She might try out the mauve ink for the diary, she thought:

Tuesday

Decided moping is dopey and Art is smarter. Bt. lots of new inks, being inkily inclined. Started my new Story + Picture Book. I think I will put in lots of rhinos as this is a good chance to draw them and they are perfect for trainee-drawers. I am excited today. I must go to the library and get some giraffe and rhino books.

I.L.Bme^w.   *I-N + B*

Giraffe poem box:
>NO GOOD GIRAFFE
>SHOULD EVER LAUGH
>IF SOMEONE NAFF
>SHOULD MAKE A GAFFE
>ANGLY GANGLY
>ROUGH AND WRANGLY
>JINGLE-JANGLY
>DINGLY-DANGLY

Underneath she drew a very small giraffe in red.

Gan-glee could be a Prince in disguise... Were there kings and queens of the giraffes? Who was it who gave the word when they all decided to sway off across the savannah? So she day-dreamed, elbows on her kitchen table. Perhaps the story itself could incorporate several rhinos. It was nearly dusk. Irena inspected her first attempt at a giraffe picture. Not bad, needed work. The Princess replaced the lids on her spicy ink bottles and lit her candle. The skin on the inside of her third finger had been squashed by her nib-holder and it was stained with ink like a school-girl's.

☙ 36 ❧

The preliminary oil sketches were completed. The Queen made it obvious that she wished to see what he had done, but Bartholomew was fearless in denying her the chance.

'These drawings are like an architect's plans. No one could see in them the building to come.'

He told the Queen that he would now need her to appear once or twice in her full splendour so that he could complete the plan for the full picture.

Queen Hephzibah felt decidedly peculiar adorning herself in her most impressive outfit, ancient family jewels and all, straight after scrambled eggs the next morning. The dressing ceremony took a long time. Once Maria had poked and prodded everything into position the Queen felt rather precarious on her stool, which up till then had been perfectly reliable.

The King came in soon after his own breakfast, as he had occasionally done before, and was rather taken aback to see his wife so arrayed when he himself was still quite informally dressed. The Queen smiled, carefully, so as not to disturb her make-up. It was some time since she had smiled spontaneously at her husband, and the fact was not lost on either of them.

That evening Bartholomew had been invited to dine privately by Julius. The Crown Prince usually preferred not to eat in the Great Hall with his parents and everybody else. On most evenings Julius found something downstairs in the Kitchens, where he could read while he was eating, or a tray would be brought to his room.

Bartholomew was very pleased. He had been briefly introduced to the Royal Children "still remaining in the country" (as their mother put it) the day after he had arrived, but he had not seen them since. Maximilian, he had learned, was away at school.

Bartholomew, still utterly confused by the Palace lay-out, was delivered by hand to the door of the Prince's quarters.

'Come in, come *in*, my dear Sir,' beckoned the Prince. 'A real pleasure to have your company.'

He poured a deep-red wine immediately. The glasses were very capacious, with designs etched on the outside, and gold rims. Bartholomew wondered how old they could possibly be, and was glad not to have the worry of washing them up.

'So how are you managing to commit the August Features to canvas? Something of a Knight's challenge, I dare say?'

He laughed, and Bartholomew smiled in reply.

'And how is my errant sister? Is she making the most of her liberty in that distant capital of the world?'

'She is in her element, Julius. Whenever I've seen her she's been obviously happy. London is full of things that appeal to her, and she seems to find pleasure in whatever she does in life. She reads for days on end.'

'I envy Tasha her courage. She just announced "I have to go," and off she went. Her Ladyship was livid, I can tell you. No one dared go near her for weeks. Woof woof. Mind you, I shall be off soon myself. I'm going to work in Paris.' He sipped his wine. 'In a laboratory. I've discovered a new species of beetle. At least, it doesn't seem to be in any of the books.'

'Beetle?' said Bartholomew. Irena had not mentioned beetles.

'Oh yes, absolutely. You see, it happened like this. One day last year …'

Julius leaned forward.

'Would you care to see my specimens, perhaps? After dinner, I mean. It's only a representative collection, the work of an earnest amateur. But I'm on my way.'

'With pleasure,' said Bartholomew, meaning it.

Dinner was arriving. Two Palace servants in livery arrived with a number of silver trays. Bartholomew luxuriated on the piles of cushions and determined to sample the full experience of being waited on like a king.

'How is it that you can escape for a whole year, then?'

'Escape is the right word, Bartholomew. The scheme has been full of difficulty. Fortunately my Father, who could easily forbid my departure, has been defiantly enthusiastic in supporting me. Otherwise it would have been impossible. And Natasha in a funny way has made it easier.'

'Would you care to see my specimens, perhaps?'

'Do you feel oppressed by the knowledge that you are to be King one day?

'I don't. To tell the truth, I might have preferred to have been born into a family where I would have been free to follow my interests more completely, but I suppose that I enjoy more practical freedom than many in my sort of position. Much more that Irena Natasha, for example. She was truly suffocating here. Her true desire is to be an artist. She can really draw, but she is diffident about her work. She seldom paints, as far as I know, but she has been drawing ever since she was a little girl. She would be shy in front of you, I imagine. What did she say about the portrait you painted? I thought it was marvellous.'

'She actually said nothing beyond asking me to bring it back when I returned.'

'Hardly fulsome praise. Perhaps she was disconcerted by it. It made me wonder what you will make of Mamma.'

Bartholomew didn't answer. He was remembering how Irena Natasha had looked at him in front of that painting in his studio. He realised that Julius was offering him vegetables. One dish he couldn't identify.

'It's called kasha. We often have it instead of rice or potatoes. Do you really like it?'

He nodded.

'That is a good sign. How long will you be with us, do you think?'

'I originally thought that one month should suffice for the completed portrait, but the pearls and sequins are going to take time, and I'm still having trouble with your mother's chin.'

'Is it so troublesome?'

'It eludes me. I have the neck, mouth and ears, but there *is* something about the chin…'

'Nothing would surprise me about my mother,' said Julius, philosophically. 'That even a painter of your attainments should come to grief over the trim of her jaw-line does little to surprise me.'

'But I shall conquer all. Have no fear. Even if my head should roll.'

'Oh, that's hardly a realistic possibility,' said Julius reassuringly. 'The axe chappie is in the Algarve for three weeks.'

'Good to see virtue reaping benefits,' said Bartholomew.

'So, unless you give Her Majesty a pointed blue nose or three eyes or something I think you should come through in one piece.'

They talked long into the night, partly light-heartedly and partly seriously. Bartholomew was thinking all along how much he liked Julius. It was not easy yet to visualise him as a reigning King, but he was undeniably a Crown Prince. He almost felt tempted to tell him everything, but…

Julius yawned, and looked at his watch. It was very late.

'If you are to do justice to the fairest in the land tomorrow, Bartholomew, we should perhaps consider some sleep. Can you find your way back, or shall I ring for someone…?'

↶ 37 ↶

The Queen's picture was not twenty feet high, but it was certainly substantial. Bartholomew had mounted his canvas on the stretcher made by his ever-cooperative allies from the basement, and had prepared the ground so that everything was ready. Today, using his sketches, he planned to block out the picture, and decide on the exact location in which to place Queen Hephzibah.

He had also been thinking hard about the background. Bartholomew had a feeling that the King would like a detailed landscape scene, with a far-distant hunting party portrayed in miniature, and, even more distant, a windmill or two and a fringe of forest. He, however, dreamed of producing a portrait that would differ from all the other paintings that might be in the Palace. He decided to take a lead from the Queen's initial pose by the tall window. He planned to paint her standing against the velvet curtain in near-darkness, with her crown, jewels and costume touched with light from a window on the extreme right of the picture. Similarly, her face, especially her eyes, would be caught by the light, so that while she appeared to stand in repose, he would be able to show the vivacity and intelligence of her expression, and more of her character besides. It was a courageous and difficult plan. The light in the window and from the window would have to be slightly ethereal.

The plan meant that the Queen now had a week off. This gave Darius a bad moment, thinking that she might try to go to England after all, but Hephzibah, caught up with Bartholomew's tantalising canvas, seemed to have forgotten all about London, Irena Natasha, and her insistence on new obedience in her children.

Bartholomew himself now disappeared from circulation. When he failed to show up in the Kitchen at lunchtime the cooks got depressed. Normally he came down at about one o'clock, starving hungry, and was bombarded on all sides with soups, homemade bread, and unidentifiable delicious things that came out of their enormous frying pans. People high and low were fed from the

Palace Kitchens throughout the day, and this meant that there was always something available for a passing portrait-painter.

Today, however, no Bartholomew. When he had not appeared by nightfall there was worried conversation. One of the boys was sent to find out what had happened to him. He made his way to the room where everybody knew the painting was going on. The door was shut. He put an ear to the wooden panel. Nothing to be heard. He lacked completely the courage to open the closed door of a room in which the Queen might be present, and was at a loss. A maid came by carrying a vase of flowers.

'Do you know whether Monsieur Bartholomew is in here?'

'No, I don't believe he is. They are not painting in there any longer. Her Majesty went riding this morning. I saw Carpenters carrying bits and pieces into the Great Ballroom not so long ago. Perhaps he's to be found in there?'

... noiselessly opened a narrow door ...

The boy ran off down the corridor. There was a great pair of painted double doors through which guests would be introduced by the Herald when there was a function, but there were also other side doors. The boy, like all the Palace boys, knew his way round everywhere, and he noiselessly opened a narrow door covered in wall-paper that no one from outside would have spotted.

Bartholomew was over in the far corner standing with his back to the door before the canvas. His tall shape seemed to be frozen into stillness, his right arm raised. The boy could see nothing of the famous picture on the easel. There was no sign of the Queen. The scene didn't seem real at all, and he was frightened. He tiptoed backwards and closed the door silently. He dashed back to the kitchen to report.

'He's painting the portrait on his *own*. In the Ballroom. He's been there since this *morning*.'

'I'm going to send something down right now. No food all day. It's indecent. How can he work?'

'But I don't understand. How can he do Her picture if She's not there?'

'I don't know. Perhaps he's starting with her feet. Maybe everybody's feet look the same. Anyway, go and find me some white cloths and cutlery. Don't forget a soup-spoon. Nobody in this building is allowed to go hungry as long as *I'm* running this kitchen.'

Shortly thereafter, the boy – whose name happened to be Nicolai – staggered up the stairs, propelling a tottering tray over which he could hardly see. One of the pages noticed him.

'Oi! Where you off to with *that* little lot?'

'Emergency supplies. Monsieur Bartholomew.'

'Right you *are*. Let me help you. He's half a mile away from here. You'll never make it.'

Bartholomew seemed to be in exactly the same position. The Page coughed.

'Monsieur. *Emergency supplies.*'

Bartholomew jumped. He turned round. His face was nearly unrecognisable, drawn and intense, his eyes deep. He saw Nicolai staring up at him anxiously, and smiled.

'No starving allowed here,' said the Page. 'More than our job's worth.'

Nicolai nodded in agreement.

'You're to eat the *lot*. Otherwise Cook will be up here wielding a rolling pin,' continued the Page.

Bartholomew laughed, and put down his brush and palette obediently.

'You know, now you've come, I *do* feel hungry,' he admitted.

Nicolai paused at the door.

'Is it true that you're painting the Queen's *feet*?' he asked.

'Don't tell anyone, but today I've been painting Her toe nails.'

↭ 38 ↭

The poor Princess was no longer quite so happy in her beloved London. She was lonely, she admitted. Fact one. Fact two was that the loneliness was definitely due to the absence of the painter Bartholomew. Having reached this conclusion she tested it in her mind, and found that the discovery was not at all unpleasant. On the contrary. What it really *meant*, was another matter, however. Could she actually be in *love* with Bartholomew? She did have the impression that she might well be. This, too, was not an unpleasant realisation.

She was lonely

But, say that were the case, if Bartholomew really wanted to marry her, could she in fact marry him? The idea of confronting her parents with such an engagement appalled her. And yet, she reasoned (not for the first time), she could never expect to fall in love with and want to marry someone of royal blood. Her mother's determined attempts in this direction highlighted its very impossibility. That meant, therefore, that there was a choice of paths open to her: to die a maiden aunt, or marry someone who was *not* of royal blood. And were she to do that, it would only be for love. Fact three. So the question that remained for her now was a small one: if this was what was going on, could she, would she (or should she) marry Bartholomew? She let herself imagine the conversation with her mother beginning "Mamma, I have some news…" And her Father, her poor Father, who would probably not be really happy with any man who claimed the hand of his Daughter, what would *he* say? She felt trembly, and sat down on her wobbly chair. What am I to do? she asked herself again.

And why hasn't he written me a letter? she continued. Again, there was nothing on the horrible, treacherous hall mat. Nothing had come since he left ten days before. Postage at home was always on the unreliable side, true, but she was slightly hurt not to have received a single envelope.

Bartholomew had now about two and a half weeks to finish the picture. There was plenty of time for her to write again. She would. One more letter. She decided to go to the National Portrait Gallery. Admire the work of other portraitists. People who completed their commissions on time. Sensitive, kindly painters, who could write letters on their own. She was certainly out of sorts, she thought.

There was thump on the door. The Princess's heart leaped uncontrollably. The unrealistic part of her mind wondered whether it could just possibly be another of her Father's equerries. She would ride pillion all the way home now if only there were an equerry's motorbike parked outside. She hurried out into the hall and it was not easy for her to manage a smile when she saw that it was Belshazzar. He grinned at her, not noticing.

I love Bartholomew, she thought then. *I love him. And that is a fact.*

'Princess,' said the composer, 'you have never come to hear my work.'

'True, O Belshazzar,' said the Princess. 'I am still full of happy expectation. I wonder, however, whether you would be prepared right now to accept a commission for a completely new composition from me? For gold.'

'Your Royal Highness, consider it absolutely done. My first commission! The ink dries as we speak. What might you require? A minuet, some symphonies, an opera or two? Do but pronounce, and we compose. Fees of extreme reasonableness.'

'Steady, Belshazzar. I need a wedding march. One, of top quality. You will be paid in gold, and you might have to conduct the one and only performance yourself.'

'Do I order a new baton?'

'Leave that to me.'

'And the symphonies?'

'I repeat: one brief but meaningful, poignant and exquisite matrimonial march. Four instruments, of your choice.'

'Title?'

'*Wedding March.*'

'Plus variations?'

'*None.*'

Later, over a coffee in the gallery, she wrote her third letter.

> Dear Monsieur Bartholomew,
>
> I have seen a thousand portraits today, but none by your hand. Perhaps, therefore, you could think soon of coming home and producing another for me? I have sufficient chocolate raisins to commission a self-portrait. Actually, I have decided that I need an art teacher myself. All young ladies should be able to draw, and have therefore been entitled to their own drawing master. I am, furthermore, afire with curiosity to learn of your relations with your personal dragon. Undoubtedly your daily timetable of jousting, rollicking and possibly even painting will have left you little time to practice letter-writing, but I shouldn't mind at all if you sent me an unpractised letter. I enclose my first, untutored self-portrait for you to wear in a cardboard locket.
>
> Know, thou most unsatisfactory of correspondents, that we do think of you fondly, in this our exile.
>
> Irena Natasha, Princess.

The Princess sealed her letter thoroughly and posted it on her way home, giving it an encouraging pat on the behind to speed it on its way.

∽ 39 ∽

The distant cause of all her worries, meanwhile, was feeling very pleased with himself. He stepped back from the towering easel, and inspected the canvas from a distance. The picture, suddenly, had begun to take shape, and he understood what it was necessary for him to do. He felt, for the first time in his life, completely confident in his powers as an artist, and with sharp anguish now he wanted to share it all with Irena Natasha. There was nothing to be done about that, however. He chewed moodily on the end of his paintbrush. Since arriving in the Palace he had, in some incredible way, hardly thought directly about her, and somehow his very first letter to her still remained unfinished. He was so bound up in the problem of producing the portrait that his mind scarcely had time to dwell on the real reason for his presence in the building. It was still all going on, however. Bartholomew knew absolutely that he loved her, but it was a private and not a public fact. He stood distractedly, thinking of her eyes and her gentle handshake at the station.

There was a noise of laughter and bustle outside the door, followed by several loud knocks. He turned round and was confronted by the Princess's two sisters, each carrying a bunch of flowers.

'Monsieur Bartholomew, we've come to invite you for a walk. It is a beautiful day and you must come and see the Gardens.'

Bartholomew bowed and put down his palette.

'I am honoured, Your Highnesses,' he said, 'but you are not to look at the picture today. It is only just beginning. I've even forbidden your Mother to peep.'

The Princesses giggled, and closed their eyes obediently.

'Come on, then. We want to know all about Irena in London. Is it true that she's become a hermit?'

Bartholomew laughed.

'Not quite. She tries to speak to another human being once a week. Through the letter box.'

'What does she *do* over there? We can never tell anything from her letters.'

'She looks at pictures. She does a lot of drawing, I think. She talks to herself, sings to herself. That sort of thing.'

'All *day*? What does she do about *cooking*? She's never learned how to do it here. Our meals always just arrive on the table. I wondered the other day what on earth I'd do about food if I got married,' said Helena.

'you must come and see the Gardens.'

'Perhaps you should order a husband who can cook? What about a tall, handsome chef?'

'Good idea. With a *sports car* and a swimming pool.'

'Oh you can get fed up with sports cars. There's no room for your legs. I think your sister lives mostly on raw apples. She is quite slender, not one of those balloon types,' said Bartholomew.

The sun was dazzling after the curtained gloom of his work place.

'Have you seen our new Aviary?' asked Helena.

'Take me to it. Who lives there? Penguins in overcoats?'

'No, silly. It's *indoor*. It was specially made for birds from *feeble countries*. Are you and Irena friends?'

'Irena Natasha is definitely my friend. We go and see things, and laugh a lot together. You can only really do that with friends, can't you?'

'I quite agree with you,' said Helena, walking at his side.

'Sometimes I finish her apple cores, too.'

'Even the *pips*?'

'Invariably.'

The Aviary was full of noisy little colourful birds of a species that he didn't recognise.

'Is Mamma *good* when you are painting her, or does she fidget?' asked Guinevere.

'That would be telling, wouldn't it...? Actually, she is very well behaved. Quite the best Queen I have ever painted.'

'Does she ask you lots of *questions*, though?' asked Guinevere. 'She usually asks male visitors the nosiest questions the minute they arrive. I can't believe what she says sometimes. Usually they don't get a chance to answer.'

'She just talks to me. I think that sometimes she finds teenage daughters a problem.'

'What, *us*?'

'She was quite clear about it, I remember. *Teenage. Daughters. A problem.* That was it.'

'Some *people*.'

'I recommended a small room in a high tower with a diet of bread and water and no spinning-wheels.'

'Oh *really*. Don't forget we would always have the option of letting down our hair.'

'Should well-brought-up Princesses really be letting their hair down in that fashion?'

'Would you rather have us experiment with kissing frogs out of the garden ponds, then?'

'I suppose that the conventional possibilities open to you young ladies are rather limited, aren't they?'

'You just cannot imagine what it is like being a Princess in this day and age. It is simply one trial after another,' said Guinevere.

'If not *worse*. Irena did the right thing,' said Helena.

'For herself,' said Guinevere. 'But it just made everything worse for us.'

'What would you have her do?' asked Bartholomew.

'Come *home*,' said Guinevere, 'so that the heat wouldn't be on us any more. When Mamma is trying to marry *her* off she forgets all about us.'

'Thank God Papa wants us to marry for love,' said Helena. 'He came and told us specially the other day. He told the same thing to the boys, he said. But it is more difficult for the older ones. One of us would only succeed to the throne if there was an *earthquake* or an epidemic or something.'

'So you are free to marry film stars?'

'Oh yuck. Not a *film* star. They're always kissing other women and getting divorced,' said Helena.

'I agree with your Father,' said Bartholomew, as they strolled on.

'Oh, aren't you already married? My Lady-in-Waiting said they're saying that you were absolutely *wedded to your heart*. I thought it sounded so romantic.'

'*Art*, it might have been, art. No, I am a poor painter of portraits without a wife in the world.'

'Well don't despair. *Some* people must like artists. To marry, I mean.'

'I trust so. Otherwise the species would die out altogether. I live in hope.'

'When did you paint that picture of Reen?' asked Helena.

'*Reen?*'

'Irena Natasha, silly.'

'Oh, *that* Reen. When she asked me if I would be interested to paint your Mother, I thought a recognisable picture might persuade your Father to choose me over a camera.'

'Well it certainly looks like our sister. It made me want to see her at once.'

'So why don't you invite her for the week-end?'

'I don't think she will ever come back here without a husband. Mamma would incarcerate her in your tower,' said Helena.

'If she does bring a husband they'll both end up in the tower.'

Bartholomew thought that would be the solution to all his

problems. He could live happily with the Princess on bread and water and paint portraits of her.

'I had better go back to work before that Sergeant-At-Arms comes after me,' he said. 'I am supposed to be earning my living.'

Reluctantly he turned back to the Palace, leaving the Princesses to continue.

'I do like him,' said Helena. 'He's funny, and not like anyone else who's ever come here.'

'So do I,' said Guinevere, 'he looks like a serious clown. Quite frightening until you speak to him.'

'I wonder what Mamma makes of him.'

As Helena was speaking, their Mother was on the telephone to her sister.

'... actually, yes, I *am* very busy. Sitting down. Not like me, is it? But it is surprisingly tiring, modelling. I have to remain immobile for hours. Looking sensitive. Yes, I *do* enjoy it... well, he's surprisingly young for such a successful society painter... mmm, *dozens*, so Darius tells me... yes, I do like him. It's a funny thing, but he's very easy to talk to... no, he just paints, frowning horribly, while I chatter on. He's a good listener, I suppose. It's a bit like seeing a psychiatrist, having one's personal artist. I feel I can tell him anything, just sitting there, while he gazes at my eyebrows, or tries to copy my cheekbones... very strange sensation. His eyes are so intense that it's slightly hypnotic. No, I don't know anything about him at all. And it's rather pleasant dealing with a young man without worrying about his *ancestry* for once, if you understand me...'

↦ 40 ↤

The secret number rang and rang. The King sounded rather out of breath.

'Irenka? Hooray!'

'I am here. How are the family, papa, and the portrait?'

'The family is fine, but nobody has seen the portrait yet. One is forbidden even to allude to it. You'll have to take it up with the artist himself. You'd like a word on progress, I expect? I'll just send someone to fetch him.'

There was a series of muffled remarks to the side partly covered by the King's palm.

'And how is my absent Princess? I am going to ask Monsieur Bartholomew to look through all our paintings when he's finished glorifying your Mother. See what he thinks. About the air conditioning for the new – ahem – *Gallery* and so on.'

Irena Natasha smiled in the gloom of the telephone box.

'Julius is packing and unpacking his trunks. It will take him weeks, and then the valet will probably just redo it. I've had them make him a really smart white coat with lapels and extra pockets. It's old silk. I hope he likes it. I was wondering what to do when it comes to unveiling the portrait. Perhaps the Dean of Arts should give an address?'

He chuckled.

'Oh, here's Monsieur Bartholomew... I'll hand you over. *Lovely* of you to telephone us. Do it *regularly*...'

There was a bump as the King lowered the receiver on to the table. The Princess strained to make out every slight noise against the background of the evening London traffic.

'Call for you,' he remarked as Bartholomew came in, and went through into the larger chamber beyond. This was where he kept his best treasures. Nobody in the Kingdom was permitted as much as to enter the room. He stooped, just inside the door, to retrieve a fallen roll of parchment, just as Bartholomew picked up the telephone and said quietly 'Hello?'

There was silence, and then he heard Bartholomew whisper '*Irenka?*'

The King closed the door behind him, and sat down on a campaign chest full of ancient swords, still clutching the document.

'*A-ha,*' he thought to himself, 'a-ha.'

'Bartholomew?'

'Princess. Your true voice in my ear at last.'

'Bartholomew, I agree and accept.'

'You do.'

'Yes. I have but yesterday commissioned our Wedding March.'

'Nice sense of priorities. What about the menu? Bridesmaids? We cannot just leave these things to the last moment.'

'I'll work on those points this evening. Page boys, do you think?'

'Definitely. Half a dozen, I would say.'

'Will you speak to my Father?'

'I *always* speak to your Father. Why should I stop now? He's invited me to look through the family art collection, by the way. Perhaps he thinks I'll pick up some hints. Thoughtful.'

'About my hand.'

'Your hand. Certainly. The moment it seems apt, I'll just slip it in to the conversation. More tea? May I marry your daughter? Leave that side of things entirely to me. You concentrate on important things like the menu. What about chilled melon with the edges of each slice cut like a castle? Any other details worrying you?'

'Not that spring to mind. I love you, Bartholomew.'

'That is not a detail. It is the whole of everything.'

'You haven't changed your mind? The world is full of Princesses.'

'I shall never change my mind. There is but one Princess in all the universe…'

Bartholomew waited until he was certain that the Princess had put down the telephone before doing the same. He sat at the desk without moving at all for a long time, oblivious to his surroundings.

After what seemed to be a safe interval the King came out of the inner chamber, and was startled to see Bartholomew still there. He stood next to him and put his hand on his shoulder.

... his hand on his shoulder...

'I *thought* as soon as I saw that painting... tell me one thing,' he said gently, 'does my runaway daughter love *you*, Bartholomew?'

'Sire, I do believe it.'

'Then, Sir, you have my blessing,' said the King, and left the room without another word.

↬ 41 ↫

The Queen, meanwhile, had no knowledge of the undercurrents that swirled about the Palace. Her picture was nearing completion, for Bartholomew was working alone for another six days, after which she would be needed for two or three final full-dress sittings. She was consequently in the highest spirits. When Hephzibah was like this the whole Palace was affected. Whistling was to be heard, the guards joked on the battlements, and all the staff breathed more easily, making sensible suggestions about things or having new ideas. Nothing further had been said lately about the *postage stamp*, though, and Queen Hephzibah resolved to mention the matter again to her husband.

Bartholomew was working alone

King Darius, on the other hand, felt burdened. He alone was in possession of certain facts that he knew would shatter the unnatural calm of their present lives. He decided to take up Hephzibah's own suggestion, and consult the Crown Prince on a matter of state.

'Julius,' began his Father, 'there is a difficult problem about which I wish to consult you.'

'I am all attention.'

'Well, it concerns the problem of your marriages, meaning all of you children.'

'Oh Father, not *that* again.'

'Well, just a minute. Let me ask you, how would you feel if one of your sisters, for example, wanted to marry someone of non-royal blood?'

'How would you feel if *I* wanted to marry someone of non-royal blood?'

'Julius, this is not the debating chamber, and I am not trying to catch you out. You will be King one day. I am curious as to your views about the other possibility.'

'Father, my views are simple. I would say that the matter was for the sister to decide herself. Unless I expire prematurely, dynastic responsibility will rest with me. I should have thought you would be more worried about my own matrimonial views.'

'That is another question. It is your sisters of whom I am speaking.'

'Well, I am in favour of their *happiness*. That inevitably entails their being at liberty to marry whom they choose. It is a tall order to expect all three of them to fall in love with the available selection of Princelings.'

'As has been demonstrated by your Mother's activities.'

'Exhaustively. There is no probably no Princelet nearer than Australia without his own dossier here. The girls are hysterically funny about it.'

'Well, Julius, I am talking here chiefly of Irena Natasha.'

'Oh, has she finally fallen for someone, then? That's a bit hard on our Bartholomew. I rather think he is in love with her himself.'

'*Bartholomew?* What makes you say that?'

'Father, one look at that portrait he did is enough. Have you not observed how he has caught her whole self with that paintbrush? He must know her face by heart.'

'That was my own instant impression. I wonder how many other people spotted it. In any case, Julius, I think it is that particular artist whom she loves.'

'Irena Natasha loves *Bartholomew*? *Really*? Well, that's wonderful. It's perfect ... But where will they live? And who will tell Mamma?'

'Julius, I have dynastic hopes of you for the Council Chamber. You have raised the indisputably crucial points. It *is* a wonderful thing. I entirely agree with you. I am less enthusiastic about the idea of being the one to inform your Mother for the first time as to their – dare we say – possible *engagement*.'

'Indeed. Mind you, Dad, she's probably got a folder on him too by now. Don't underestimate her. But what do we really *know* about him?'

'Nothing factual at all, in my case.'

'Me too. His parents are amicably divorced, he told me. But they are rich, I believe.'

'That is certainly one point that will find favour with his – dare we say –possible *mother-in-law*. Hmm. Well, enough for now, young Julius. We will talk more of this... Meanwhile...' He held a finger to his lips.

Darius next summoned the Minister in charge of the postal service for the latest bulletin.

'But, Your Majesty, how can we start work on our designs until we have seen the picture itself?'

'Don't be idiotic, man. The artist is internationally famous. His portrait will undoubtedly *look like Her Majesty*. You know what Her Majesty looks like, don't you?'

'Indeed, Sire, I am in that privileged state.'

'Well then, you can start designing accordingly, can't you?'

The Minister nodded noncommittally. Darius realised he had been unreasonable.

'Look, just have a think about some possibilities. I'll make sure you see the portrait the minute the curtain goes up.'

Bartholomew, meanwhile, was still in a daze. He had not slept at all during the whole night, but lain on his back with his hands behind his head, staring and thinking and dreaming. He just could not take in what had happened. At first light he had a wash and took himself firmly back to work.

The picture stared coolly down at him. It was almost alive, but not quite. He knew that he could give it life but that he would have to tread delicately. He had coaxed and bullied the portrait into being much as he had treated his model. Today the Queen stood within the shadows, waiting for him to beckon her out. He frowned at the work in hostility, trying consciously to dominate it, but it was too late. The Queen's own strength was already in the paint, and the unfinished portrait seemed about to cry out "Marry my daughter? *You?* Never, never, never!"

He turned away to mix new whites. There was still a lot to do, but he had already achieved more than he realised. Some of the painting seemed to have completed itself while his mind was far away. His coffee was cold, and there was a lump of paint in it.

After what he had promised, Her Majesty would be expecting her picture to be ready in a few days. He bent once more towards the dark canvas.

❧ 42 ❧

'It's OK, Your Majesty,' said Bartholomew with no warning a few days later. 'It's all yours.'

'You mean by that to say, Monsieur, that my portrait is finished?'

'All but the signature and a coat or two of varnish later. You are free, Ma'am, to come and criticise.'

Bartholomew bowed low. He felt triumphant, although to the Queen he looked white and strained. Hephzibah, too, found herself quite nervous on hearing this announcement. Somehow she had anticipated that the unveiling of the portrait would be slow moving, and marked by ceremony. She stood up, smoothing down her clothes, hesitating to approach.

'I'll leave you, perhaps,' said Bartholomew. He put down his equipment and quietly left the room.

Queen Hephzibah approached the back of the easel very reluctantly. She stood for a moment with a hand on the wooden frame, aware that she was on the brink of a significant step. *This is silly*, she thought, and put her head firmly round the edge.

At first sight she thought that Bartholomew had played an elaborate joke on them all. The whole of the great canvas seemed to have been painted gleaming black and nothing more. This dampening impression, however, was a trick of the light. As she stood directly in front of the canvas she came to realise how much Bartholomew had accomplished over the weeks. She saw her own face there within the darkness, clever, striking and determined, the eyes shining and alert. And there was more beyond. Something also showed of her frustration, imperiousness, even disappointment. But these were things in her that were hidden, not shouted out. And here they were, somehow written in the corner of her eyes or mouth. Bartholomew, scrutinising her for so long, had seen much more than the mere cut of her profile.

She felt shocked, as if surprised on her throne without any clothes on by a roomful of people. Yet, as she looked deeper, she felt that there was a further level in the paint; the artist saw her and understood her, she thought, but he also liked her.

She began to inspect the formal details of her picture, and marvelled at the soft light that streamed between the heavy velvet curtains, their thick tumbling folds forming the right side of the picture. The light fell delicately on her crown and old jewellery, and drew sparkles about her hair, at her neck and wrists. The girl within her marvelled to see the intricacies of her own dress, how blobs of colour came together to reflect the complex patterns in the lace. *How does he do that?* she wondered.

'How does he do that?'

And, as she gazed even more intently, she knew that there was admiration and affection within the painting too. The Queen felt hot and disturbed, and, at the same time, profoundly flattered. Monsieur Bartholomew, she thought, had certainly done her a royal portrait.

Bartholomew had not waited to learn the Queen's verdict, and there was no one to be seen when she stepped into the corridor. Hephzibah wanted to find her husband at once. He had gone riding, she found out, and would be back at four o'clock. The Queen had to change out of her finery, so she decided to wash her hair and think about something else altogether.

King Darius was red about the cheeks and exuberant on his return. He was fond of riding, and today had galloped a long way in the wind on his favourite horse, and back again at almost the same pace. Going upstairs to change he found a note from the Queen. She was taking tea in a small sitting room below and would be very glad of his company.

'Darius,' said the Queen happily, pouring tea, 'it's finished.'

'Is it?' said the King distractedly. He was eating cake ravenously, and thinking of ordering something more substantial too. 'Is it really? 'Bout time too.'

'Darius, could I ask for a moment of your undivided attention?'

'*Entirely* undivided, is that? Seems rather a tall order.'

'Darius, the *portrait* is finished.'

'The *portrait* is finished?' He put down his plate. 'Why on *earth* didn't you tell me? What are we doing here spilling tea if that portrait is somewhere in this building, finished, and available for inspection?'

He stood up hastily, scattering crumbs.

'Lead me to it, Your Majesty.'

They went together, hand in hand, off to the Ballroom.

↝ 43 ↜

King Darius was wordless. He stood, still hand in hand with Queen Hephzibah, and gazed at the painting in the corner of the State Ballroom. The Queen watched him out of the corner of her eye and observed the change of expression as he gradually understood what Monsieur Bartholomew had achieved with his paintbrush.

hand in hand

The King sighed deeply and looked at his wife. It was a long time before he spoke.

'This is utterly remarkable. I think, my dear, that you must feel flattered. He has really painted your portrait, hasn't he? It's very odd: when you look at it first you see nothing, just a dark indoor scene. And then you begin to see my Queen. I'm very proud of it. I've never seen such a picture in my whole life. I'm very proud of you.'

The Queen put her arms round her husband.

'I'm very excited about it, she whispered. 'I *am* flattered. He is an extraordinary person. He is a true artist.'

'Do you like him?' asked Darius. 'From this it looks to me as if he likes you.'

'I do. I like him and respect him both. One strange thing about him is that when one talks to him, one forgets one is a Queen. I mean, there is a directness about him that produces a similar feeling in oneself. It is peculiar to be closeted with a portrait painter. It is impossible to hide, because they are there to depict you in detail. But with Monsieur B. I still felt comfortable despite the scrutiny.'

'You know the picture he painted of Irenka?' asked the King softly.

'Yes, of course. That startled me when I first saw it, too.'

'I understand from something that he told Julius that he painted it from memory, not from life.'

'*What*? How can he have?'

'Julius says he must know her face by heart. *I* think your Monsieur B. is in love with her.'

'Bartholomew? With Irena Natasha?'

'Yes.'

'Are you sure, Darius?'

'I am.'

'Oh dear. I think we ought to feel a bit sorry for him. Irena is scarcely likely to recognise that his qualities more than make up for his status. She's hardly the sort of Princess who would marry a society painter. It's rather a pity. I would have thought that if anybody of that type might prove to be a potential husband for her, he could be the person. You know, Leepy, I've been thinking a good deal lately. It is far from probable that all three of our girls will ever accept card-carrying Princes. Some of those we've seen recently do defy description. And happiness is what is important after all. I do feel sorry for Bartholomew if you're right. Maybe it will blow over.'

'Well, actually-'

'She's probably long since met someone in London, if not married them on the quiet. I've always feared that she would marry someone hopeless the minute she arrived there just to make her point. It's one of the reasons I was so opposed to her going there at all.'

'Actually, Hephzibah, that may not be the case.'

'*What?*'

'I believe that Irena Natasha loves Bartholomew. They will be wanting to get married, I imagine.'

There was a very long silence indeed.

'Darius, I need more tea. At this point tea is completely crucial. We will talk further downstairs.'

The King bowed to his wife's portrait, and she waved to it in acknowledgement. They retreated politely, hand in hand, and went back downstairs. They were walking quite sedately, but the King couldn't help noticing that the Queen seemed rather breathless.

༝ 44 ༝

Bartholomew didn't feel at all like cleaning his brushes. He decided to go and see if Julius was to be found.

'I am glad to see you, Bartholomew. I've been meaning to mention something to you. Father is officially *in favour*. So am I. That's one King and one King-to-be who are on your side. I am sure the girls will feel the same way. Maxi, too, when he's back.'

'On my side?'

'With the Irena thing. I think you only have to ask him about the details. Her hand. You know the kind of procedure.'

'Julius, are you sure?'

'Oh yes. We have discussed the matter more than once in complete agreement. I cannot tell you how pleased I am about it. There's just the question of the drag - of the Queen. Your – ahem – future Mother-in-law.'

Bartholomew swallowed.

'Julius –'

'Father thought it probably all depended on how the portrait goes down. How have you managed with the chin?'

'Her Majesty is looking at it now, I believe.'

'The portrait is *finished*?' He stood up. 'Why on *earth* didn't you tell me? What are we doing here idling about if that portrait is somewhere in this building, finished, and available for inspection?'

The King and Queen sat side by side on the small sofa. Unusually, Darius was pouring the tea himself.

'Try this for the inner woman.'

'Is this really *happening*, Leepy?' asked the Queen faintly, although not as faintly as she might have wished.

She was in a most unfamiliar position. Hephzibah felt that she ought to disapprove of what was going on, emphatically and volubly, but she found that she couldn't. At all.

'I've an idea,' said the King, 'We could make Bartholomew a Grand-Duke, or something. In acknowledgement of his services to Art and Crown. We could find him a bit of land. A few cottages, couple of retainers. What do you feel?'

... pouring the tea himself

'To tell the truth, Leepy, I don't think it matters. Now that you have told me, I cannot find it in my heart to put my foot down, although I know I ought to. Does Bartholomew know what your views are, or is he expecting to be thrown into our deepest dungeon on multiple charges of having the cheek even to think of marrying our absentee daughter?'

'I intimated to him the other evening, rather subtly I think, that he wasn't to feel too apprehensive on my account.'

'Really? What did you say?'

'Er, I think I told him that if Irenka really loved him and he really loved her they had my blessing.'

'Subtle indeed. I wonder that he grasped your meaning.'

'It's in here,' said Julius to his sisters, outside the Ballroom. 'It's over by the window. Come and see.'

'Do you not think that we should not have some kind of Official Occasion,' said the Queen rather later, 'to celebrate the Unveiling of my Portrait?'

'I quite agree. And look, why don't I send a telegram to Irena Natasha inviting her to the party?' said the King.

The Queen nodded.

༒ 45 ༒

It was something quite out of the ordinary in those days for a telegram to be despatched from the Palace, and the process involved many more people than just writer and recipient. The King's pencilled note had been received by the Chamberlain, who undertook on his own authority to write it out neatly in capital letters. This version was entrusted to a reliable messenger, whose responsibility was to hand over the message safely at the Post Office. There it was checked, and laboriously typed out on the new machine, under the careful eye of everybody who happened to be in the Post Office that morning (most of whom could read large writing upside-down with ease). So it came about that everybody in the Palace, the Capital, the surrounding Countryside and, before long, the entire Kingdom knew that Bartholomew's painting of Queen Hephzibah had been completed, and that the King had politely summoned his daughter Irena to come home for the party.

That party, everyone knew, was going to be more than a modest affair. The underlying plan was for as many people as possible to enjoy themselves as much as possible.

The Party Committee meeting was just underway where there was a thundering rap, and the Queen put her head round the door.

'Ah, *there* you are, gentlemen. Is this not a meeting about my party?'

'Er – yes, Ma'am. The Chamberlain here and I were just – that is, we thought that we would save you –'

The Queen came right in, closed the door and sat down.

'Good. I've got a preliminary list of essential names here…'

Some time later a London postman named Albert, clutching a telegram, rang the Princess's doorbell for the third time. There was still no answer. What was he to do? Albert was seventeen, and this happened to be his first week in employment. Although he had read the rule book carefully he had completely forgotten what was to be done with a telegram that couldn't be delivered in person.

Taking it back would be absurd. Probably the lady (he had naturally read the envelope, and thought that the word *Princess* on it was a joke) was out at work, and would be home soon. If he manoeuvred it professionally through the letterbox she would see it on her return. Otherwise it would be a whole day late. The postman made up his mind, and slid the flimsy sheet through expertly.

Albert was not to know, but at that minute the lady in question, accompanied by a small suitcase and a large volume of poetry, was sitting upright on a slow train travelling slowly across Europe. She had departed very early the previous morning, on the spur of the moment, leaving only a note for the composer with her forwarding address. She would be needing the manuscript of his music as soon as possible, she said, and the gold would be all ready for him as promised.

sitting upright on a slow train

↭ 46 ↭

Darius had the idea that now would be a good time to show Bartholomew the family paintings and drawings. He had by no means exaggerated to Irena on the subject; there truly was a large collection, and it had been years since the King (or anyone else) had been on a tour of inspection.

'Vanya, could you find Monsieur Bartholomew and bring him to me? And we will need keys for the upper floors of the West Tower, if you could dig them out for me?'

Vanya looked surprised.

'The Tower keys? Prince Julius has them already, Sire. He collected them this morning. I think he's up there now with Monsieur Bartholomew.'

'Yes, I see him.'

'Ah,' said the King. 'I see. I'll have to follow them up there then.'

He made his way across the courtyard to the West Wing. Access to the Tower happened to be from a small discreet room like a broom cupboard. The door was ajar. The King pushed it open and started to climb the stairs. It was so dusty that he could clearly see the fresh imprints of two pairs of shoes mounting above him. Most of the rooms off the staircase had been used for storage as long as Darius could remember. As he climbed he heard voices from above, echoed and amplified by the round stone walls. He heard one voice say, indistinctly 'I think he's gone under here,' while the other replied 'Yes, I see him. Be careful, be careful.' The King smiled to himself. It was not a difficult matter to recognise what was going on.

He made deliberate noises as he approached the door. Stepping in he saw Bartholomew lying flat on his stomach peering under a chest of drawers. Julius was on his hands and knees to one side, peering underneath in great concentration. Neither entomologist was aware of his presence, so the King stood quietly. At length Julius stood up and was greatly surprised to see his Father in the doorway.

'Oh, hello, Father. He's escaped I'm afraid. A beautiful specimen. The longest legs. Even Bartholomew admired him.'

'Your Majesty,' said Bartholomew, scrambling to his feet in confusion.

'Gentlemen, let me not disturb you. I had merely the idea of introducing Bartholomew to the family holdings of other artists' work. I have no desire to disturb you in the scientific pursuit of knowledge. There can be little doubt that no one has been up here in a decade, and these rooms are likely to be the playground of many enchanting species.'

'Exactly, Father. It didn't occur to me until this remarkable fellow waddled idly across the floor under our very noses. I just want to get a good look at him.'

'Shall I then take Bartholomew up to a higher storey or two and whet his appetite?'

'Do by all means. Although he has the making of a first-rate specimen hunter. It was he who suggested the stylish pincer movement that we were just putting into action.'

'Won't the thing just die of fright?'

'Hardly. Few are that sensitive. Some go off in a sulk until you stop looking at them. Most just ignore you altogether.'

'Well, Monsieur B., shall we go up?'

They reached a chamber directly above. Bartholomew could hear Julius still whistling encouragingly to his unwilling spider. The room was packed with pictures, stacked against the walls in rows, more or less according to size.

'Nobody, not even Vanya, knows what we have up here. No idea at all. There's no list, or catalogue, just a few papers and receipts from the last century. There are at least four rooms-full like this. And then, of course, all the portraits around the Palace. Those you might have noticed. I imagine?'

'Indeed, Your Majesty. A mixed bunch, if I may put it so.'

'Some are definitely mouldy, in more ways than one.'

The King began to go through some of the nearby paintings, and before long the investigators were on their knees, coughing and spluttering as they disturbed the settled dust.

'Your Majesty,' said Bartholomew, wiping the hair out of his eyes with blackened fingers, 'there is something I should like to ask you.'

'Certainly, Bartholomew, certainly. Go ahead,' said the King, wheezing slightly.

He was on the other side of the room, sitting on the floor, with a great frame laid across his knees. He had been breathing on the glass and polishing it with his handkerchief, trying to decipher the painter's signature. He looked up. Bartholomew's pale face was temporarily disfigured by a broad sooty band.

'I should like, Sire, if you will not consider it presumption, or even a capital offence, to ask for the hand of your daughter Irena in marriage. I love her, and she has given me to understand that she -'

He broke off in confusion. The King was sitting back, laughing heartily.

'Sire,' said Bartholomew in panic, 'if I have offen –'

'Don't be daft, Bartholomew,' said the King. 'It's just that you look like a zebra, and I was imagining what the Queen would say if she knew that her daughter was going to marry a zebra. Of course you have my consent, man. If our Irena loves you as you say, then her Mother and I will be truly happy to welcome you to our menagerie – I mean ménage – as –'

He burst out laughing again.

'Perhaps before you dance with the Queen on breaking this happy news you might contemplate investing in a bowl of soapy water and a big sponge. I have the horrible feeling that your stripes will be contagious at close quarters.'

Tears were beginning to run down his cheeks at the idea of his immaculate Queen waltzing around the ballroom with her brand new chimney sweep of a son-in-law. He dabbed at his eyes with his hanky and blew his nose.

Bartholomew looked up and exploded into laughter himself. The King's face had been transformed by the hanky into that of a second zebra. He pointed at the King speechlessly, and rolled on the floor in agony.

Julius appeared in the doorway, confused by the hilarity.

'What on *earth* is wrong with you, gentlemen?' he enquired, before he caught sight of his near-unrecognisable Father in the corner. He looked at Bartholomew, and back at his Father, and slid to the floor himself, dropping the spider and helpless with laughter.

༒ 47 ༒

Darius, in the bath not long after, was talking through the open door to Hephzibah, who was sorting absentmindedly through her jewellery box.

... talking through the open door ...

'... and then he formally asked me, with great charm, for Irenka's hand,' recounted the King from under his loofah.

The Queen stopped rattling beads and looked up attentively.

'And what, pray, did you answer, Your Majesty?'

'I treated his question with the mature gravity it deserved, and, speaking thoughtfully on behalf of the two of us, fully aware of the great family lineage that stretches back into the remote past,

I welcomed him into the bosom of our family. It was a solemn moment for us both.'

'You have done well. I think, though, I shall delay offering him the maternal cheek until Irena Natasha materializes. Talking of which, there's still no response from her? It's always inconvenient when one is working out numbers and planning the catering, not to know who's coming and who isn't to a party.'

'I don't know what has happened. Hopefully she'll call tonight. But since we are inviting at least twice as many guests as will fit hygienically into the Ballroom at one time I imagine that we could probably cope with an Irenka, even if she turns up at the last minute. She probably won't eat things in measurable quantity, either.'

The Queen smiled.

'True. But I would be glad to know that she will be here in time.'

'So will Bartholomew. But I haven't told him about the telegram, by the way. I thought I'd wait until we've heard.'

The truth was that the Princess, quite unaware of the imminent portrait party, was stuck in another train on a branch line somewhere hundreds of miles away. Fallen trees were being removed from the track before repairs could be put into operation. Her last-minute food rations and drink had almost run out. Luckily two enterprising villagers came to the train windows from their farm, so she was able to buy fruit and milk for a few coins. The journey was supposed to take about thirty-six hours, but it was already more than forty-eight hours since she had left London behind her, and after this delay there was still a smaller train needed to carry her over the border of her own Country.

The Princess sighed. She had read and re-read all the poems in her book and written one or two herself inside the back cover. She had made all the railway-carriage drawings she wanted. She was planning a new story about a boy in a signal box during a storm. She was also beginning to wonder whether it might not be a better idea to get out and *walk* home.

⌘ 48 ⌘

The morning before the party the King thought to invite the Dean of Arts to drop in and inspect the portrait, intimating that he might care to make a small speech at some point during the celebrations. The Dean arrived immediately, secretly hoping that the picture would be a disaster, and that he would be called upon at the last minute to paint the Queen's likeness and save everybody's face. He was very taken aback when the Chamberlain conducted him over to the easel.

... that painting ...

By this time the famous easel had been cleaned up and itself painted entirely in gold to match the great frame, but the Dean scarcely noticed the trimmings. The Queen's face seemed to look right at him and say

'Oh, it's *you* is it? And you thought you could do Me better!'

The Dean found himself going red and muttering an apology, but the Queen, austere in her splendour, continue to look at him sardonically, and he couldn't evade her eye. He just wanted to escape from the room, but as the Chamberlain was still standing next to him he had to keep gazing admiringly at the painting, making remarks like "Magnificent technique!" or "He leaves the Old Masters standing!"

At length, it seemed appropriate for him to withdraw, and the Dean was careful to thank the Chamberlain appreciatively for his time.

'What,' he thought to himself, 'could I *possibly* say in a speech with that painting in the room listening to me?

∽ 49 ∽

People started to arrive at the Palace grounds the very minute it could be truthfully said to be getting slightly dark. The long drive from the outer gates was decked with lights, and servants were stationed at helpful points to help out the older guests in their very best clothes.

The Princesses Helena and Guinevere had, of course, spent the entire day being attended in their wardrobes, and their labours had certainly borne fruit. Meeting his daughters near the Audience Chamber Darius was overwhelmed.

'You look like... *Princesses,*' he concluded.

'We *are* Princesses, silly,' said Helena.

'Oh yes, so you are.'

Bartholomew had been dressed by Julius. All he had brought with him from London were the sort of clothes that didn't show paint, and in any case he had nothing to his name that was remotely suitable for a formal Palace party. Julius, on the other hand, had 'dressing-up' clothes in abundance, and poor Bartholomew spent much of the afternoon standing about in his underclothes while Julius and his valet burrowed in cupboards and wardrobes and emerged every minute saying "Try this!"

By now the artist was close to unrecognisable. He wore a white silk shirt with frilly centrepiece, and an old shapely blue silk waistcoat with four elaborate pockets and a separate collar. Over this went a black velvet frock coat, while a broad red sash went across one shoulder, and he had velvet breeches, white satin leggings, and a pair of buckled shoes that would normally only be seen in a museum.

Bartholomew stood bashfully in front of the Prince's huge, blotchy mirror, and ventured the satirical suggestion that he really ought to have a sword. The valet, at a nod from Julius, disappeared at once. Julius found an old paintbrush from a family box of watercolours and tucked it in the red sash across Bartholomew's chest, creating him *Painter by Appointment to the Crown Prince* there and then.

The Crown Prince himself was utterly resplendent in blue velvet and was just putting the finishing touches to his own complex waistcoat buttons when the valet returned carrying a pair of matching silver swords.

'These are technically duelling swords. They were last properly used in September 1789, when one of His Royal Highness's distant great-uncles was slightly insulted by a visiting ambassador, and had to take satisfaction from him the following morning.'

'Oh yes, those,' said Julius. 'They're quite sharp still, aren't they, Zbigniew?'

'Assuredly, Your Royal Highness. You could rely on them implicitly should the necessity arise.'

'Comforting,' said Bartholomew.

'Comforting,' said Bartholomew

Zbigniew was affixing one of the swords to his outfit as he spoke. It was the first time that Bartholomew had worn a sword of any description since the age of five. He experienced a momentary surge of military sentiment. 'What on *earth* would Irenka say? Would she even recognise me? Why, oh why, isn't she *here*?'

Two trumpeters with silver trumpets stood, one each side of the double doors that opened on the Great Ballroom. The Chamberlain had the task of welcoming each individual guest by name. The King and Queen had their small travelling thrones set up near the windows. The room was illuminated by a series of great chandeliers, enhanced on all sides by candles. Bartholomew's painting was shown up by a narrow light that shone down from above. The Queen had wanted her picture to be veiled at the outset, with the veil to be removed following a volley of cannon-fire on the battlements. As it was, the effect of the arrangements was that the picture was the first thing seen by anyone who entered the room, and the Queen could not, in all honesty, claim that she was not satisfied by the perfectly extraordinary impression it created.

The court orchestra, instruments gleaming with polish, were installed on a specially decorated podium fringed with golden railings, and waiters in their best costumes were to be seen gliding about the room with trays of all kinds. Tables laden with foodstuffs were set up in the many parts of the Palace that had been thrown open to the visitors. No visitor could remain hungry for more than five minutes.

The area near the portrait was especially crowded. Naturally each visitor wanted to see it close up, but each found that it needed more than a two-minute glimpse, so after a while there was quite a wait to get anywhere near the easel.

High court officials circulated gracefully, introducing people to one another, or to Monsieur Bartholomew. Bartholomew stood with his back erect, and answered endless questions about the portrait, declining commissions to paint dogs or children, and regretfully declaring that he could not take on apprentices in his studio.

He noticed Julius coming towards him with a glass of champagne. The Crown Prince winked broadly.

'No duels for tomorrow yet?'

Bartholomew's hand, unconsciously, was resting on the pommel of his sword.

✌ 50 ✌

An hour or so later the phone rang in some distant passageway. Vanya, seeking fresh serviettes, happened to be nearby. He lifted the receiver.

'*Yes.* Your Royal *Highness.* What a *pleasure.* Yes. Vanya… Fine… Thank you, she's very well. I've seen him in the last ten minutes. There's a bit of a do on here this evening. I'll just fetch him for you.'

He laid the mouthpiece carefully by the telephone, and signalled to a boy messenger. It was Nicolai.

'Fetch His Royal Highness Prince Julius out of that Ballroom at the double and bring him to this telephone.'

Nicolai vanished.

'What is it, Vanya? Why all the excitement?'

'It is the Princess Irena Natasha. She's home, at the railway station beyond the pass with no currency. There are no taxis and she doesn't feel able to explain to the Station Master who she is.'

Julius laughed and picked up the receiver.

'*Irena Natasha.* Wonderful! Stay *right* there. We'll be there in an hour. Find somewhere warm and read a book.'

He grinned at Vanya.

'Not a word to a soul, *least of all* to Bartholomew. Keep the party ticking over till we're back and we'll start all over again. Nicolai, get your coat and your sword and we'll go together to rescue our Princess.'

They ran off to the stables. Julius called to the duty ostler to hitch two horses to the small coach that his parents used for afternoon spins, and sent someone ahead to open the gates to the outer world. It was fresh and cold and he felt full of strength. He swung the boy up on to the seat on top, and was about to jump up himself when Vanya slid out of the shadows, carrying a blanket and a cloth-covered basket. Julius stowed the supplies between the seat cushions inside the carriage, jumped up on top, grabbed the reigns, and they were off.

The horses, it seemed, sensed the urgency of their mission, for they galloped out into the night with their breath sharp in the

178

cold, their hooves rattling on the cobbles, out beyond the Palace walls down towards the distant pass far below. Nicolai held on for dear life and looked up at the eager face of the heroic Prince beside him, staring ahead, whistling between his teeth, and concentrating in the darkness. The coach bumped and swayed beneath them, the golden wheels spinning and flashing in the moonlight. The boy thought to himself that to a watcher in the field the delicate painted chariot dashing madly through the night must look like something out of a fairy tale.

They saw the Princess through the window, huddled inside her jacket, sitting by her solitary case in the station waiting room. She was half frozen and more than half asleep. The horses panted and steamed outside as Julius and Nicola quietly opened the door and went in to collect her. Nicolai opened the basket. Inside there were sandwiches and cake, a flask of tea and a bottle of cordial from the Cook. Julius took his sister's hands and kissed them, rubbing them in his own.

'Irena Natasha, welcome home,' he said. Nicolai bowed, unwrapping a sandwich for her.

'Come,' said Julius, 'you can eat in the coach. We must return. There is someone who would like, I think, to see you. Nicolai will look after you.'

Nothing at all had changed when they returned to the Palace. There still seemed to be hundreds of people wandering around, and the orchestra was still playing with undiminished energy. Julius took the Princess down to the Kitchens. The Cook, forgetting all propriety, dropped whatever she was holding and squeezed the Princess so hard that she couldn't breathe. Julius judged that his sister was in safe hands, and went off to find Bartholomew.

The artist was still surrounded by eager questioners. He too looked exhausted. Julius made his way over to Bartholomew, and whispered something in his ear. Bartholomew disengaged himself courteously and followed the Prince to the door.

'Bartholomew, you look oppressed by admirers. You need some fresh air. Go up on to the ramparts over the portcullis where the view is always exhilarating. I'll come up and join you in a moment.'

Obediently Bartholomew turned to climb the stairway that led up to the battlements above the gate. He felt hot and wearied, and glad of a moment's tranquillity.

...he knelt on the ancient stone before her.

Julius ran down the stairs, three at a time, to the kitchen. Without remark he grabbed the Princess' hand and led her up the staircase behind him, up to the ground floor, and then pointed to the upper staircase.

'Go up there,' he whispered. 'Go and get some oxygen. It's quite safe. Someone will come for you.'

Irena Natasha obediently started to climb the old worn stairs. She trod lightly, one step at a time. She felt curiously peaceful and relaxed. It was hard to believe that she could be home. She had been travelling for days and days and she-

'Irenka!'

Bartholomew stood there against the ramparts, outlined against the liquid dark. Incredibly, thought the Princess, he seemed to be wearing a sword. Bartholomew's heart pounded, and he could say nothing further. His Princess stood before him, smiling, and he knelt on the ancient stone before her.

∽ 51 ∽

...for a long country walk...

The following morning, after late breakfast, the Queen was adamant that her husband, every one of her children, and anyone else who could "legitimately claim to be connected with her in any way" should be dragged off for a long country walk on the slopes above the Palace. This proposal met with surprising enthusiasm. There was a good deal of hunting for sensible footwear and hats, but eventually the Royal Party assembled in the Front Hall, to be led off energetically by the King and Queen.

Helena and Guinevere marched on either side of their sister, hungry for news.

'Do you *like* it there?'

'Are you going *back*?'

'Have you found a *husband* yet?'

'Taking those enquiries in order, *yes, yes* and *yes*.'

'You *haven't*! Who *is* he? Does *Mamma* know?'

'Her Husband is discussing things with him at this very moment.'

'What are you saying? Not *Bartholomew*?'

They ran like greyhounds and jumped like monkeys on the unsuspecting artist.

'This is no way, if I may say so, to treat a new member of a Royal Family,' said the King, helping Bartholomew to his feet. 'Please excuse us, ladies, we gentlemen have much to discuss.'

They moved on ahead, deep in conversation.

'When you are married,' the King was saying, 'I do hope that you and Irena will spend as much time as possible with us. I quite see that you will have to *live* abroad, but I would like to suggest - if you can arrange things conveniently - that you and Irena spend a good part of the year here. It will give us a lot of pleasure to see you both, and more peace and quiet when you are not here,' he added in a low tone. 'Now, I wouldn't expect you both to sit about here and do nothing, but I was wondering what you would say if we were to build an Art Gallery here for our people, and take all our neglected pictures and put them on exhibition. You both could take charge of all that, and maybe look out for new pictures for us when you're away. We have always needed a National Gallery, and what better time to build one, and who better than you two to take charge of it? Also, I suppose that if you don't think we've got anything good enough, you can always paint them yourself. What do you say?'

'Your Majesty, the idea of building a new gallery seems to me sheer inspiration. It is brilliant. And I wouldn't dream of trying to carry Irenka off for long, either. We will have to see what she thinks of the plan, of course.'

'Quite so. But you might put the idea to her when the moment presents itself…'

Julius found himself striding out beside his mother.

'Good stuff, this. I have to say I couldn't approve more. I wonder when they will be married.'

'Certainly not straight away,' said the Queen. 'They have many things to sort out, and we have to discuss where they are to live, what will happen about money, and all those things.'

'But you are *pleased*, Mamma?'

'Julius, to tell you the truth, I don't think that things could have possibly worked out better for your sister. She is a lucky girl.'

'I think also that my brother-in-law-to-be is a lucky man.'

'Yes, I believe that he will be able to cope with her.'

'Mother, you are an incurable romantic…'

'I *thought* he loved her,' said Helena. 'There was something he said once before. I thought it at the *time*.'

'Nonsense,' said Guinevere.

'Does this mean that *we're* off the hook with regard to Princes?' continued Helena.

'Maybe you are. Actually, I've been thinking. I think I'd rather prefer to marry a Prince after all,' said Guinevere.

⌘ 52 ⌘

Princess Irena Natasha was now unpacking her London suitcase. Everything inside was terribly crumpled (and it *was* agreeable to be wearing one of her old dresses for a change), but her story book was still safe and flat on the bottom and the ink had not run at all. She found some tissue paper and wrapped the little book up carefully. She was just writing Barth- on the front cover when there was a knock on her outer door. It was Vanya, with a roll of paper on a cushion tied with ribbon. Vanya offered her the cushion, remarking,

'I am instructed, Your Royal Highness, to wait for an answer.'

The message read:

'Princess mine (if I dare thus address you), am I permitted to speak to you alone?'

Irena Natasha wrote:

'You are. Come at once. I wish to give you my inky present.'

They met, at Vanya's suggestion, in the Small Music Room. The Princess sat by her future husband in the window seat.

... by her future husband ...

'This is for you,' she said. 'It is my first work. No other eye has ever lighted upon it. I have decided to do pictures that go with words and sometimes words that go with pictures. London to me is full of both. I have been practising and practising while you were away, Bartholomew. When we go back I think I might, with your help, now seek out a Drawing Master.'

Bartholomew nodded, undid the package and slid out the little book. The Princess watched him apprehensively. The cover, inked in fine capitals, said:

THE HEAD TO TAIL AND IN-BETWEEN TALE

OR

HOW TO KNOW YOUR STATION

OR

DO NOT GET ABOVE YOURSELF

OR

THE PURSUIT OF HARMONY

Bartholomew turned the pages in utter silence, reading every single word, and inspecting all the Princess's drawings.

'I love it. I love every syllable and every line. And *all* the titles. You must publish it. It is perfect.'

He laughed, and pressed the volume on which she had lavished so much care to his chest with both hands. The Princess laughed aloud herself and kissed his hands. They sat there together without moving. Bartholomew thought then that this was a good moment to bring up the Art Gallery...

'... we must obviously agree to this plan, and work out how much of the year we must spend here with them all.'

'I cannot do my work here, Bartholomew. No-one here will ever take it or me seriously. I have to live completely away from here, with you. I am totally committed to our freedom to work and create together. But not *here*. We must live in London in a perfectly freezing garret where we can – ...'

'Irenka, I could not agree more. But until we are safely wed with all the papers to defend us, it might perhaps be advisable if we played ball and were not too *militant*... They can always throw me in one of the family Dungeons, if I put a foot wrong. I mean, Princess mine, we could be *firm* and *independent* and *private* and everything... er... *later*...?'

∽ 53 ∽

Then it was tea time. The servants had made up a large fire in the grate, for the evenings could still be cold, and the old chamber was very convivial. There were two ornamental cakes that had survived the onslaught of the night before, and some delectable sandwiches.

Then it was tea time

Everyone was relaxed with teacups or lemonade when Queen Hephzibah leaned forward and said into a sudden silence,
'I suppose we can take it that you will be coming *home* now, Irena Natasha?'
'Nothing of the s-'

'We have a plan, Your Majesty, approved by the King,' interrupted Bartholomew swiftly, putting down his teacup, 'that we will spend part of our year here administering the new Art Gallery, and part living abroad working on its behalf, promoting it and collaborating with artists and dealers. There is the question of our own work, too. Commissions abroad, our various projects…'

Irena Natasha looked at her Father.

'You mean that you really will found a gallery with all those ghastly canvases?'

'Absolutely.'

'Then that sounds like a perfect arrangement.'

She smiled secretively at Bartholomew, her Husband-to-be. The Queen looked quizzically at her Husband, remembered her portrait, and smiled at Bartholomew graciously.

'So that's all right then,' said Darius.

He burst out laughing, and threw his crown up into the air. It gleamed as it twisted in the fading sunshine through the windows and fell, to be caught by the King with a dextrous flip of his outstretched hand.

'This seems to be an absolutely unbeatable solution. *Everybody seems to be happy.* I think I must congratulate myself on the nimblest piece of diplomacy I have ever achieved. I have found the way, my dear Irena Natasha, for you to become the Princess who sometimes does come home after all.'

Epilogue

Prince Julius was swaying about in a taxi, his first ever experience of such a vehicle. He had stepped from the train in Paris in a state of wonder, and had remained in total exhilaration ever since. Despite his Mother's admonitions he had eventually travelled without an attendant, and with the minimum of luggage. He was wearing one of the strange new three-piece suits that the King's own Tailor had made for him, and since it was rather too warm for a Parisian spring day, he was looking forward to getting out of it. The taxi swerved into a small alley, and screeched to a stop outside a long, low brick building.

'Voilà, M'sieur.'

Julius struggled with his bags on to the pavement, and handed some unfamiliar coins to his driver, who sniffed and drove off without a word.

The building had but one entrance, with a shabby painted door marked with a faded sign. He could just make out "…-*boratoire*" in worn green letters. Julius felt fit to explode with excitement. He rang the bell firmly and waited.

The door opened slowly, and a boy put his head out.

'Oui?'

'I have come to Paris to work with the Professor.'

'Un moment.'

The door closed. Julius waited patiently. The door opened again and a convincingly professorial head appeared.

'Vous êtes Monsieur Jules?'

'Er, oui,' said Julius.

The Professor flung open the door widely with an extravagant gesture of welcome.

'Bienvenu!' he beamed. He was rotund and humorous, mischievous as well as scientific-looking.

'Jules, you are very much awaited indeed for our humble *laboratoire*. We have all been looking forward deeply to your arrival. Here is your workbench. Here is your seat. Here is little Carlo, who cooks and washes up and does everything else. Here is my daughter Francesca, whose handwriting, I believe, you already know. Oh, and there is a *telegram* for you. It came just ten minutes ago. I hope it is nothing serious.'

Julius put down his bags and looked around the laboratory. It was exactly as he had envisaged it. He looked at Francesca. She was, in fact, slightly more beautiful than he had envisaged. He felt wonderful.

He felt wonderful

Julius picked up the telegram unenthusiastically. He noticed in despair that it was addressed "His Royal Highness the Crown Prince Julius, % Professor..."

He opened it, even less enthusiastically.

Dear Julius,
   Hopefully this telegram will find you as it leaves us, in high spirits. Irena Natasha and Bartholomew are to be married *next week*. Father says can you please come home *at once* for the Celebrations. Sorry for the inconvenience. It will only take a fortnight out of your schedule, at the most. He says to tell you that he promises to build you a Natural History Museum for your Twenty-First Birthday Present if you come back. Just wait until you hear the *music* they're planning. I heard the orchestra practising, just a few bars, and ran for my life. And as for the *composer* she's brought over… If he thinks he's going to marry Guinevere or Helena he's got another think coming….
   Everybody still loves my portrait, even the postmaster. They all send their love.
   Your loving Mother,
   Hephzibah, Queen of all the… etc. etc.

Julius put down the telegram slowly, and breathed out deeply. Francesca came over to him.

'Is it true that you are really a Crown Prince?' she asked hesitantly.

Julius nodded gloomily.

'I'm supposed to be in *disguise*, but now you all know the worst about me in my first five minutes.'

'Oh, that's all right, Jules,' said the Professor comfortably, 'it's nothing to be ashamed of. Even royal entomologists can feel at home in this laboratory.'

He opened a folder on the bench, hospitably.

Julius laughed, little Carlo clapped his hands, and the beautiful Francesca smiled shyly at him in welcome.

- The End -

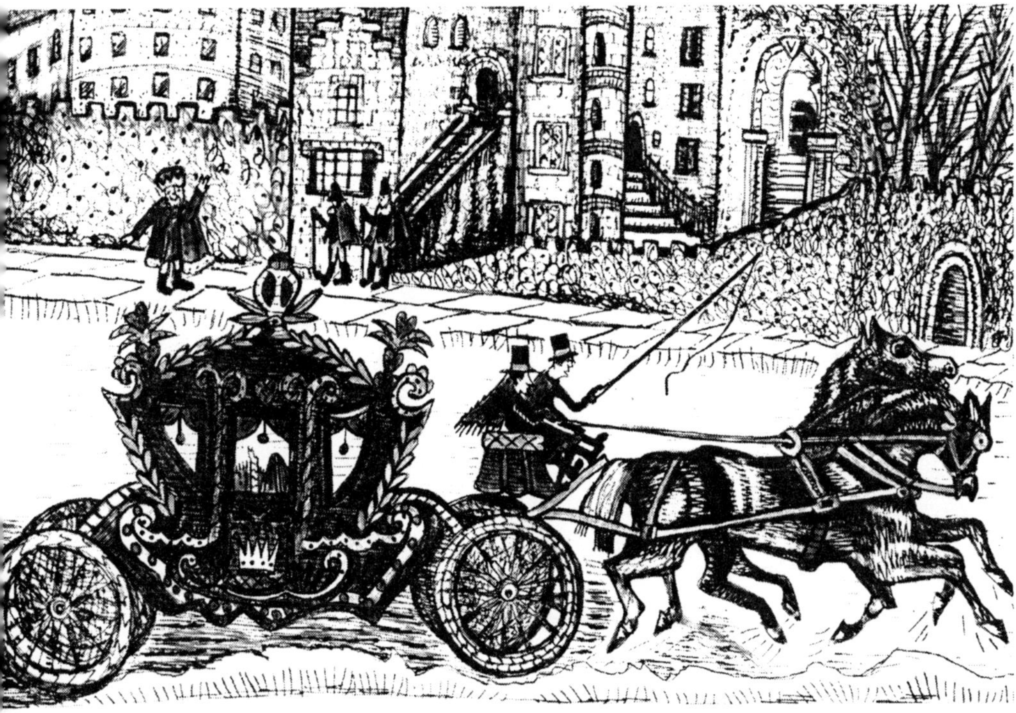

Printed in the United Kingdom
by Lightning Source UK Ltd.
136158UK00001B/121-138/P